CROWN OF BONES

Book Four - Crown of Death Saga

KEARY TAYLOR

I hope you
enjoy these
books as
much as I did
♡ Shelby

CHAPTER 1

I REACH FOR CYRUS' HAND, SEARCHING FOR SOMETHING solid and real to ground me. I need reality, not this insane altered version where I have over three hundred half-siblings flooding into the city I love.

Just as I reach for him, just as I feel the warmth of his fingertips, the ground shakes.

Sharp shards of wood, concrete, and glass fly through the air.

The boom is deafening.

Instinctually, everyone curves in on themselves. They shield their eyes and ears. Screams rip through the crowd and the already chaotic street.

I turn, my eyes wide and searching.

The building I was in just moments ago, the one I interrogated Lorenzo in, is now a smoking ruin. Flames lick into the sky, the timber frame smoldering.

A bomb.

Someone just set off a bomb.

I reach to the belt slung around my waist, and sure enough, the one I'd taken from my private armory is gone.

"Lorenzo!" Cyrus bellows. I've never heard so much anger and malice in his voice. "Find Lorenzo! Do not let him slip away if you value your way of life!"

It's as if nothing ever happened. As if all these Royals never saw their King decapitated. Like they never believed him to be dead for an entire month. Every Royal within earshot leaps to action.

I meet Cyrus' eyes with horror.

He escaped. Lorenzo, the man who quietly plotted our demise for over six hundred years, escaped.

I dart forward, colliding with Cyrus, burrowing my fingers into his shirt.

"He slipped away?" I ask in anger and horror.

Cyrus' eyes rise to scan the crowd, but he places his hands over mine, giving a small squeeze that I think is supposed to feel reassuring. "My grip slipped as the bomb went off," he says. And I hear the anger at himself in his voice.

"The timing was no coincidence," I say with malice. "Someone set it off as a distraction."

I whip around, my eyes searching the crowd. Through the smoke, I find Malachi racing toward us with focused, ready to fight eyes.

"I want you to bring me Lorenzo's children from here at Court," I growl.

I swear, I feel heat rising from my eyes, they're so brilliant red.

"Yes, my Queen," he says, immediately turning back into the smoke and disappearing.

My eyes wildly search the space around me. My heart is beating a thousand miles an hour. I feel like I can't get enough oxygen into my lungs. It's like there are walls around me, but they're crumbling, caving in on top of me.

Lorenzo is planning to end our world. He just confessed to me his two goals: to make sure Cyrus' reign is over, and to unite all vampires. If that means exposing us to the humans, if that means the eventual rule over them, so be it.

He's just escaped.

I had him. And he's gone.

Too much.

It's too much too fast.

It's too bad. It's all falling apart too fast.

Leave, my brain screams at me. *Run. Far. Fast. Forget this place. Go live somewhere far away. Take Cyrus and leave it all. Imagine how happy you could be away from all of this.*

There's a word echoing in my brain. There's a tunnel, long and dark. At the very end of it, I see a hazy shape. No, a face.

Sound presses in on my ears. It's a word, repeated over and over.

I blink, and the tunnel dissolves.

It's Cyrus, and that word is my name.

"Logan," he says. His voice sounds desperate, terrified.

I blink again, and again. I take two quick breaths, but realize I was beginning to hyperventilate. I stop.

"I'm…" I stumble over words. "I'm okay. I'm okay."

The scared but relieved look in Cyrus' eyes tells me he doesn't quite believe me, but he gathers me into his arms, crushing me to his chest in an embrace.

"I never should have made you deal with all of this on your own," he says into my ear. "Forgive me, *im yndmisht srtov.*"

Click.

Something in me slides back into place.

Click.

Click.

I shove my fear aside.

I brush away the pile of debris on top of me.

I stand straight.

I roll my shoulders back.

I can do this. I can do this because I'm not alone. "Thank you," I say, reaching for Cyrus' hand. When we should be going and fighting or making orders, or something, he's here. We're together, and I feel it, I am the center of Cyrus' entire world.

"Thank you," I barely breathe the words again as I meet his eyes.

Oh, how I love those eyes. I see something spark in them. Something deep. Something possessive. Something dangerous and powerful.

He drags me back to him, kissing me deeply, claiming my soul as a part of his, giving me his own.

We aren't even two, anymore.

We are one.

Cyrus and Sevan.

Logan and Cyrus.

Shouts around us drag me back into reality. I break the kiss and turn, searching the clearing smoke for signs of return.

But there is no one. So I step forward, heading down the road.

"Matthias," I yell into the smoky day. "Matthias!"

I hear a shout, someone else yelling the General's name. A moment later, Matthias comes running up the road.

"Was that what it sounded like?" he demands. When he sees Cyrus, he slows, stopping in the road. There's a mix of awe and suspicion in his eyes.

"A bomb," I say with a nod. "Lorenzo St. Claire is missing. I'm sure you and your men have noticed the crowd about to head into the valley?"

We'd been distracted, just moments before the bomb went off. Because as soon as we stepped out of Lorenzo's interrogation, all eyes had turned to the canyon. It was far, but our vampire eyes are strong.

There, as if waiting for an order, were dozens and dozens of Lorenzo's children.

Matthias turns, looking toward the mouth of the canyon.

"You have the numbers," I say. "Take every man you can spare, and use any means necessary to make sure those people do not get into this valley."

Matthias slowly turns back to me. "People? My kind or your kind?"

"Our kind," Cyrus answers.

Matthias glares at the two of us. "What kind of numbers are we talking about?" he asks. I see it in his eyes: he doesn't like this. There's anger building under his skin, and he looks ready to rage.

"There are one hundred up there, right now," I tell him. I have to be honest. "But we expect two hundred more to be arriving soon."

Which takes the numbers down to seventeen to one.

"You're asking our men to take a huge risk," he says, his eyes narrowing. "We came because Dorian and Malachi assured us that the numbers were staggeringly safe." Matthias takes two steps forward, standing nearly nose-to-nose with me. "You can only expect us to do so much for money, take so much risk for money. Jeopardize so many lives for money."

Cyrus takes a step forward, pushing a hand against Matthias' chest, pushing him out of my face. "You ally your-selves with us, because this is about to become a *real* war. A real war fighting for the safety of your race. You fight with us so that you may have a safe home to return to when all of this is over. You fight now to *live*."

Matthias' eyes grow slightly wider and wider with each of Cyrus' words. I smell the sweat prickle out onto his skin. I hear his heart rate pick up.

He *should* be afraid.

Because though they came here to pretend, to carry out a fake take over, they have no choice now but to fight in a very real war that will affect the entire world.

"Gather the men you need," I say, fixing him with a confident stare. "Do not let them into the valley."

There's a moment's pause. A hesitation. A consideration.

But he gathers himself. He offers a nod, and turns to return to his troops.

As I watch him go, I feel it: this is the end. The end of my plan. The end of our time in sorting things out. We don't have time to sift through the loyal now.

The time to declare is now.

"Cyrus?" a breathy voice says.

I look to the side to see a woman sink to her knees. With wonder and awe in her eyes, she stares up at Cyrus. "We thought..." her voice quivers. "We thought you were gone. We thought you were dead."

"Your King still stands," Cyrus says, holding his chin high. Another man walking through the village stops, his expression slackening. He changes course, dropping to kneel beside the woman.

"My King lives," he breathes.

The word ripples through the village with physical power. I hear it whispered all around us. I hear voices spreading the word.

King.

The King lives.

Others step outside of buildings, searching up and down the road.

And they gather. Those who have already been released. I told Dorian we had to wrap up this investigation, that we needed to utilize those we could trust—now. So as the word spreads in just moments, the street fills. Soon there are ten kneeling around us, all staring at Cyrus with eyes full of wonder and awe. Then there are twenty. Thirty. They stand along the edges, looking at a miracle and evidence of the strength of curses.

"I grant unto you my deepest thanks for supporting your Queen while I recovered," Cyrus says. He has to make a speech. They wait for his words with baited breath. They crave it. They're silently screaming out to him, begging for answers. For reassurance. "This has truly been a unique time, as our Queen has ruled on her own, amidst so much turmoil and uncertainty. No other in our history," he says as he turns to me and raises my hand to his lips, gently pressing them to the back of my knuckles, "has ever been more prepared to lead our kind than she is."

Cyrus' attention and focus may be on me, but the crowd that surrounds us has eyes only for their King.

The same as I do.

"How?" someone asks. I look out, finding a man with tears brimming in his eyes. "How can you be alive? You were…" He can't find the words to declare what happened to Cyrus a month ago.

Cyrus lifts his chin and turns back to the crowd. "Long ago I was cursed," he says. His eyes fix on the horizon, and I know the vision that is playing out in his mind. "Cursed for my ambition with the craving of human blood, the blood of what I once was. I was cursed to lose the woman I love most, over and over, for taking away her free will."

I squeeze Cyrus' hand, a support. A confirmation. That yes, he did an awful, cruel, terrible thing. But I forgave him a long time ago. I love him still today.

"But the opposite end of that part of the curse was that I was cursed to never, ever die," Cyrus says again. His voice drops an octave, a level in volume. His gaze falls to the ground. "That while my wife would die over and over, I could never, ever die. I could never escape punishment."

There's so much regret in his voice. So much pain. The weight of the moon is in his voice and on his shoulders.

"I have been staked through the heart dozens of times," Cyrus continues. "I have been sliced nearly in half on multiple occasions. I have been cleaved through the head another time. And just a month ago, my head was severed from the rest of my body."

The focus suddenly returns to Cyrus' eyes and he looks around at the crowd. "At this point, I have to believe that there is no extent of damage that can be done to my body that will permanently put me in the ground. I am immortal, to every extent of the word."

There's fear that creeps into some of their eyes. And I understand it. No one, no matter how good or evil they may be, should truly be un-killable. It just isn't natural, even in our terms. No one is invincible.

But Cyrus is.

As I scan those who surround us, I also see awe. Respect. Reverence.

This is their king, and he is an invincible genesis predator.

"I may have lain there vulnerable and exposed for weeks," Cyrus continues. "But my wife never gave up on me. Sevan," he turns to me, and my heart flutters. "She protected me always. Guarded me. And defended our city while every-thing tried to fall apart."

He reaches out, caressing my cheek. And for a moment I

forget that we aren't alone. That it isn't just the two of us, and that there is an army around us, that there was a bomb detonated just a few hundred yards from our home. That there's been a plot to destroy us growing for centuries.

It's just Sevan and Cyrus.

But he looks back at our descendants, and I'm pulled back to reality.

"This army is not our enemy," Cyrus says. The crowd has grown as he's spoken, as those released, gather. "They have aided Queen Sevan in rooting out traitors. They have been instrumental in preserving our way of life. Our city. It may have been carried out under a guise, but desperate times call for desperate maneuvers."

This is where I watch the people closest. This is where I search their faces. Where I watch their hands. Where I look for bending knees and alighting eyes.

I see one there. Out on the edge of the crowd. And there. A woman kneeling among the others.

"Big things are coming," Cyrus says as his eyes turn toward the canyon. The others look, as well. And we can all see it. The army marches across the valley. A moving avalanche, sliding toward the mouth of the canyon. "Things will change. And now is the time to declare."

Their eyes flick back to Cyrus, uncertainty and questions slackening their lips.

"Will you stand with the crown and defend our way of life?" I say, speaking loud and strong. "Or do you end your time of peace and stand with the betrayers?"

It's dead silent for about five seconds.

And then that man at the back of the crowd looks toward

the mouth of the canyon. He stares at it for several long moments.

Suddenly, a woman kneeling among the crowd springs to her feet. She darts toward the edge of the crowd, aiming in the general direction of our invaders.

But she doesn't get five steps beyond the ring before she's tackled by no less than five Court members, who immediately tear her limb from limb.

My heart races. A feeling surges inside of me.

Hope.

Pride.

Love.

I look back at the man who looked curiously toward the canyon. But he looks back at me, meeting my gaze. He swallows once. And then he nods, as if saying, *I worry, but I stand with the crown.*

"Come," Cyrus says loudly. "You are needed at the castle. We must prepare."

Without another look at them, Cyrus turns and begins walking back up the road, toward the castle. Hand in hand, I walk at his side, matching him step for step.

We're halfway there when I see Malachi shift in the shadows, staring out at us from beneath a hooded cloak.

"We will join you in the Great Hall shortly," I tell the crowd following us. "Go on."

There are a few nods, and the crowd continues up the road toward the castle.

"Have you found them?" Cyrus questions his grandson.

Malachi's expression darkens, and he shakes his head. "All four of them somehow escaped while you were interrogating Lorenzo. We believe it was one of his children who set off the bomb, allowing Lorenzo to escape."

I swear under my breath, looking around as if I expect to see half-siblings creeping along the shadows.

"And there is no sign of Lorenzo himself," Cyrus concludes with a hiss.

Malachi shakes his head gravely.

Cyrus doesn't rage. He doesn't tear anyone's head off.

He lets out a slow breath through his nose and rolls his shoulders back.

"Come, you are needed at the castle," he says. "We need to make preparations. Find Dorian and meet us there."

With a nod, Malachi immediately slips back into the shadows.

CHAPTER 2

THERE WERE THIRTY-SEVEN ROYALS GATHERED AROUND US just ten minutes ago, listening to Cyrus' speech, but here in the Great Hall there are only thirty-six gathered.

It's a man. One who was standing along the outside edge. Not the one I was concerned about. Just another man who had listened quietly.

But now he's gone, and I fear I know exactly what has happened to him.

He's turned against us.

I try not to think about only that man over the course of the next hour, but it isn't easy to let it go.

Once Dorian and Malachi arrive, Cyrus dives right in. He does not beat around the bush. He explains everything as far as we know. That Lorenzo St. Claire, a man born here at Court, who has lived among us for so long, has been conspiring against the crown for hundreds of years. Cyrus tells them Lorenzo plans to bring an end to the separation of

Born and Royal, that he wants to usher the world into a new, exposed light.

Tactically, I drop numbers. I won't let them forget how outnumbered we are in the world. I have to make them understand the fear Cyrus and I felt when we were once hunted.

We explain it very clearly, there are a hundred Royals who have been brainwashed by Lorenzo their entire lives standing just outside our city, and there are more who will be arriving any minute.

And when they are all gathered, their numbers will very, very nearly equal our own.

Then it is time for me to fully explain the truth of why the army is here. That I used them to make people expose their truth. I utilized them in unearthing those who betrayed Cyrus, leading to his decapitation. I confess it was all fake. But it did uncover those who had betrayed us.

I expected them to be angry. To look at me with bitterness. And some of them are. But as Malachi had predicted, most of them look at me with reverence and respect. They see the brilliance of what it accomplished.

I see it when they look from me to Cyrus. And I know Lorenzo was right. Cyrus and I, we really are two sides to the same coin in many ways. I might not use bloodshed like Cyrus. But I can be cunning when needed.

"We would have fallen within days if I hadn't done what I did," I explain, holding my chin high. "I have to believe the only thing that kept Lorenzo's descendants from flooding into our city immediately was the fact that they could not communicate with him. They had no way to know if he was dead or alive, or if they should still have come. The conspirators would have tried to seize control of the castle within days, and they probably would have killed me, and countless others who would have stood at my side."

Some stand straight, and I see devotion in their expressions. I know some of them doubted my ability to lead them on my own, but they still would have stood by my side if it came to a fight.

"You know everything now," Cyrus says. He reaches for me, wrapping an arm around my lower back and resting his hand on my hip. I look at him, and in this moment, I feel like we're so exposed. Like at any moment everything we've built is going to evaporate and everyone in the world will turn against us. Any moment, it's just going to be us against the world again, just like it was thousands of years ago.

"So with all of the cards in your hands, with all of the crucial information," Cyrus continues. "You have a decision to make."

It's absolutely silent. Every one of those thirty-six people watch us, hardly even breathing.

"Do you wish for things to remain the same?" Cyrus asks. His throat is thick. His words are slightly strained. "Do you wish to be safe in secrecy, do you want to remain among the loyal bloodlines? Or do you wish for the world to evolve into something entirely changed where all the lines will blur?"

Cyrus stands straight, tilting his chin down, looking out over the crowd from beneath his lashes. His lips are set hard, and I swear, power is radiating from his eyes. It blankets the

Great Hall, fills every centimeter of the space until there isn't even room for air.

"Declare yourself now," Cyrus says with such clarity. "Do you stand with us, or Lorenzo St. Claire?"

Dorian and Malachi immediately take one step forward. With a balled fist, they swiftly bring it to their chests, right above their hearts.

They will stand with the crown.

Another six men and women repeat the pledge, and Cyrus and I nod to each of them in thanks.

Another ten follow suit. And then the rest of the room pledges.

My heart is full of gratitude and pride. I can hardly contain it. But I don't let the emotions that well in my eyes break.

"Thank you," I breathe, looking to each of them. "It means so much. You all are our family. I love you all. Every one of you, even if we don't know each other yet. You're my family."

I hope they can feel the full depth of my words.

I see nods. I see looks of pride. I see love radiating back.

I know Cyrus might not feel that same love toward them. I think the extent of his love died when our son died his human death. The only being he truly loves anymore is me.

But he is loyal to our kind.

"We need your help," Cyrus says, moving along. "If there were time, we would have finished this through investigation. But that time has run out. We need to end it, today, and so we must rely on all of you."

"You know each other," I say, taking a step forward.

"You know your family. You know your friends, your neighbors. You've talked behind closed doors with them for decades, for centuries. If there is anyone we may not be able to trust, we're relying on you, for the safety of our kind, to tell us. And you may release those you know will stand with us."

They look at one another, and little murmurs echo throughout the Hall.

"We will meet you all back at the castle gates at midnight," Cyrus says, once more taking my hand. "With all our brothers and sisters, we will make a plan to make our stand."

With one more look at my descendants, I smile sadly, knowing nothing is going to be the same again.

Already, I feel the tides shifting.

Hand in hand with Cyrus, we turn, and walk out of the Great Hall.

I'm tired. Like, really, really, really tired.

As if sensing it, Cyrus guides us toward the stairs and we rise up to the second floor.

I hesitate, looking down the hall, toward where I know Eshan's room is.

"I need to get my brother out of here." The words come out in a blurted realization. "What's about to happen here... It's no place for a sixteen-year-old human boy. He isn't safe here."

"Where would you send him?" Cyrus asks.

I hesitate, considering for a moment. He can't go back to Colorado. There's no one there for him with our parents gone. I consider cousins around the States. But considering what he's been through? What he knows? How is he ever supposed to fit in with normal people again?

"I think Elle would take him," I say as a light bulb turns on. I consider the warm, soft woman who is kind of my aunt, the mother of my cousin. Cousins. "She could keep him safe. I don't know if Ian could ever get over his resentment of us, so I can't send him to Alivia. But I think Elle would take care of him."

"I know she would," Cyrus says, placing his hands on my shoulders.

I feel guilty. Because of me Eshan doesn't have parents anymore. I said I would take care of him. But I realize now, I can't do it. I'm not ready. And I can't be the guardian he needs when I'm trying to fight a war.

It breaks my heart.

He may not be blood, but he is my only living family left.

The guilt in my heart is enough to choke me.

"Would you like me to call her for you?" Cyrus asks.

I shake my head. "I can do it."

CYRUS GIVES ME PRIVACY IN OUR BEDROOM AND I SIT staring at my phone for forever without making the call. Once I do, there's no taking it back.

"Hello?" a sweet voice with a Southern accent answers when I finally find the nerve.

"Elle," I say as emotion suddenly springs into my eyes and my voice threatens to crack. "It's Logan."

"Logan," she says in surprise. "Is everything alright?"

I sniff, trying to hold in the tears that want to roll down my face. "Not really."

"Tell me what's the matter," she says.

In the background I hear the sound of children fighting and then a male voice intervening. I smile, imagining Elle's life in Boston with her husband with the weird name of Lexington, and their three kids. They are tied eternally to a house because of their oldest daughter, who in reality is not Lexington's. But for now, they're separate enough for their kids to have a childhood.

"There's a lot going on," I say as I relax back into the headboard and the pillows. "A lot of information will be going out to the Houses in the next week or so, but you just need to know that Roter Himmel isn't a very safe place right now."

"What can I do to help?" she asks. I hear a door close and the background noise is shut off.

I sniff, holding in the tears. I don't want to have to do this. I don't want to send my brother away. He's my best and only friend here, besides Cyrus. He's my last link to my normal, human life, before it all spiraled into something huge and deep and heavy.

"It isn't safe here for my brother," I finally say the words. "There's going to be a lot of fighting going on here very soon. And he's too fragile. I can't risk him getting hurt or killed, or used against me."

My voice grows shakier with every word I speak. Tears finally break free, rolling down my face. I put a hand over my mouth to keep from sobbing.

"We'll take him," Elle says. She does it without hesitation. Without conditions. "He'll have to share a room with George, but as long as he doesn't mind stories about farts and dinosaurs, I think they'll get along just fine."

"Really?" I ask, but the word cracks and is barely audible.

"Logan, you're family," Elle says. "And whatever is going on there can't last forever. You two will be together again."

A breath of relief slips past my lips.

She's right. I hadn't thought of it that way, that this is only temporary and I swear to myself I won't let this new war last forever.

"Thank you, Elle," I say. I'm welling over with gratitude. "Can he come soon? Like, as soon as I can get him over there on a plane?"

I swear I can feel her soft smile through the phone. "Of course. I'll tell Lexington he needs to go buy a bunk bed."

I huff a laugh, smiling so big my face nearly hurts.

"Thank you," I say again. "I'll send you his flight info so you can pick him up."

"You're welcome," Elle says. "You take care of business."

We say our goodbyes and I stare at the wall for a moment after I hang up.

This world is filled with bad people. But there are also some really, really good ones in it, too.

Now I have to do something I really don't want to.

I walk down the stairs and head down the hall toward Eshan's bedroom. I find the door already open, and to my surprise, Cyrus is sitting on the end of the bed, talking with him.

I stare at the two of them, my eyes wide, it's such a bizarre sight.

I have a sudden flash back to Cyrus with our son, trying to council and advise him.

And here he is with my human brother.

"Boston, huh?" Eshan says, giving me a slightly wary look.

Those stupid tears are instantly back in my eyes. "I'm so sorry, E," I nearly begin sobbing as I sit on the bed, wrapping my arms around him. "I just can't stand the idea that you might get hurt with all this shit going on. I'm supposed to take care of you, but all I can do right now is keep you safe and out of harm's way."

My brother gives a sigh and squeezes me. "Don't go getting all hysterical on me, geez," he says, and I can practically hear his eye roll. I sit up, studying his face, trying to read him. "I mean, I'd rather stay here and help you, Logan. But I've seen what some of these guys can do, and frankly, I don't really feel like getting ripped limb from limb. So yeah, I'll go live in Boston for a while."

"Really?" I ask with a tearful smile.

He actually does roll his eyes this time. "Really, you drama queen."

I'm so relieved he doesn't hate me. I just shake my head and hug him once more.

"Let's get your bag packed," Cyrus says as he stands and looks around for one. "We should leave as soon as possible."

My emotions swing all over the place as the three of us

work to pack what little Eshan brought with him from Colorado just over a month ago. I really am a mess. I'm scared. I'm relieved. I feel guilty. I feel grateful.

Together, all three of us head to the highest tower at the back of the castle.

We certainly can't drive to the airport with all of the descendants of Lorenzo swarming the mouth of the canyon.

But times have certainly changed since I was last at the castle as La'ei.

A shiny black helicopter waits in the middle of the landing pad. A pilot waits there, as if he has nothing else in the world to worry about, other than taking the King wherever he wishes to go.

Eshan can't stop saying how cool the ride is, even in the darkening night. He's a total sixteen-year-old boy right now. I hold his hand, laying my head on his shoulder, just relishing in this last moment I get with him.

We touch down directly at the airport, and the pilot is already waiting to spirit my brother away.

"This isn't goodbye for good," I say as Cyrus hands him his backpack.

"I know," he says, giving me a little smile.

"You'll be extremely, overly helpful for Elle and Lexington, won't you?" I ask as I pull him in for a hug. "They're doing us a huge solid by taking you in, considering they have three little kids at home. You'll be a crazy helpful big brother, won't you?"

"Are you kidding me?" he says as I release him. "After enduring fifteen years as a little brother to you, I think I can handle being the big brother for once."

I smile and Cyrus clears his throat, looking over at me, letting me know it's time for him to leave.

So with a sad smile and a promise that this is only a *see you later*, we say our goodbyes, and I watch my baby brother climb into the airplane, and then take off into the sky to safer grounds.

CHAPTER 3

I LIE IN BED, TRYING NOT TO THINK ABOUT ANYTHING.

Not about my brother flying across a continent and an ocean. Not about the army down in the valley. Not about the invaders.

I lie on my side, and I look at the ring on my left hand. The gold band looks dark in the eleven o'clock hour, the diamonds only shine a little, and the center emerald looks pitch black.

But here, on my finger, is the symbol of the one bit of happiness I have right now.

The bed dips and then there's a warm body spooning up to mine as Cyrus lies behind me. He wraps one arm around my middle, pulling me in tight to him.

But I keep looking at my ring, letting a moment of happiness and relief spread through me.

"Tell me about the wedding you always dreamed about as

a girl," Cyrus breathes into my ear. "Tell me all the details so I can bring it to reality for you, Logan."

I smile. Just the sound of his voice sends waves of goosebumps washing over my skin. His nearness sends electricity cascading down my body.

"Would you believe me if I said I never did have any kind of wedding fantasy?" I ask.

"No," he says with a smile in his voice. "I don't know that I would."

I laugh, continuing to study the facets of my emerald. "It's true. I never had any grand ideas about my dress, or where the location would be, the flowers." I roll back toward him a bit so that I can look into his dark eyes. "The groom."

Cyrus takes my hand and brings it to his lips, pressing a kiss to the ring he placed on my finger only a few days ago.

"I could marry you in the grossest strip club in Vegas, wearing jeans and a ripped t-shirt, and it would be exactly what I want, Cyrus," I say. "Because you'd be there, wanting to marry me for some insane reason."

When the words come out, I realize how much I have changed in the time I've met this man. Just four months ago I never would have said that sentence. I could never have lain here, so vulnerable and open and honest. My bitter heart just couldn't be real like that.

Yes, I have multiple other people in my head now, the memories of eight dead queens.

But I think people evolve when they become one like Cyrus and I have.

They change.

For the two of us, I feel like it has been into the better versions of ourselves.

"You may not have any imaginings of the day, my love," Cyrus says, leaning in just a little closer, studying my eyes. "But I have thought about the day for weeks now. The day you will be my bride."

The word sends a thrill through me. It's scary. That's for damn sure. Because—me? A bride? It's so real. So binding.

"I have thought about you in a white dress, Logan," Cyrus whispers, leaning in. He teases his lips along my jaw. "I have thought about those two words slipping past your lips." He presses a soft kiss to my skin, and I barely even hear the words *I do* as my eyes slip closed and my body sparks to life. "I have thought about a ring on my own finger, the first I will have ever worn."

His kisses slip, beginning to trail down my neck. "I have thought about the night alone that will follow," he purrs as he kisses his way down my neck. My back arches and I roll as he shifts on top of me. My right knee falls to the side, inviting him between my legs. "I have thought about this skin." He nips my neck just a little with his teeth. "I have thought about every inch of it."

My hands rise up, finding the hem of his shirt. My hands slip underneath. His skin is warm, covered in goosebumps.

It's agony. I'm touching him. I'm here in this bed with him, breathing the same air, hearing the words I crave. But it's not enough.

It's not enough.

Cyrus' hand goes to my thigh, sliding up until he slips over my hip, and then to the hem of my own shirt. His rough hand caresses my stomach. And finally his fingers hook on the edge of my bra, lingering.

"I have fantasized about every inch of your skin, Logan," Cyrus whispers into my ear, his lips teasing the skin there.

I wrap my legs around his waist, and I feel like I'm in pain, I want every part of him so bad. That little decision that I never gave clear acknowledgement to in the back of my brain, the one to wait until after the wedding, shatters to pieces, evaporating into the air.

But through the night, a shout cuts through the dark. Followed by another.

We're both on our feet in a fraction of a second, looking out the window.

There's fighting down in the streets. The people yell, no, scream, at one another. I see one man swing at another. I see fangs bared. I see brilliant red eyes.

There's a group of ten surrounded by a crowd of nearly a hundred. They back down the road, toward the lake.

There are others that look cornered.

There's so much screaming.

So much fighting.

Through the stairways and halls Cyrus and I bolt and not a minute later, we plow through the front gates.

The shouting and sounds of fighting intensify.

Cyrus grabs a woman as she runs by, nearly knocking her off her feet. "What is going on?"

Her expression is livid and she doesn't even look at Cyrus, she's in such a rush to get back into the thick of things. "More than thirty of us have decided they want to side with Lorenzo," she says. "They're trying to leave the city."

More than thirty.

I see Cyrus' expression slacken and he loosens his grip on the woman, who instantly darts back to the fight.

That's…that's nearly ten percent of the residents of Roter Himmel.

After everything, after this entire interrogation with the army, there are still so many who have decided to turn away from us.

As I turn to the fight once more, I realize it isn't just a fight.

It's a painful betrayal. A turning of backs.

It's pleading and begging.

These are their family members. Their friends.

This is Roter Himmel being torn apart after centuries of bonds and relationships.

The loyalists will fight.

But can they kill?

Do I want them to?

I clutch my hands to my chest, feeling my heart being shredded.

How can we ever survive this? How will our world ever, ever look the same after all of this conflict? After all this splitting?

Your world will never look the same.

The man who beheaded Cyrus had said those words. And he was absolutely right.

My world has come to an end as I knew it.

Two individuals break free from the crowd, and with a speed that is nearly invisible to the eye, they dart out across the valley.

Another five follow suit.

I realize that they didn't just escape.

My people let them go.

The group of ten makes a break for it, and they're chased, but only for so long.

Neither Cyrus nor I do anything about it, as over the next ten minutes, we watch the loyalists drive the deserters out of Roter Himmel.

I count every one of them as they leave us.

Fifteen.

Twenty-four.

Thirty-two.

And then the town turns quiet. Faces grow solemn.

They all turn toward the castle instinctually, and every one of their eyes falls to us, none of them knowing what to do now that thirty-two of us have turned their backs.

"Everyone inside the castle," Cyrus says.

CHAPTER 4

It's kind of beautiful, really. In all my lives here at the castle, we have never, ever done something like this, been this united, relied on one another so much.

Every resident of Roter Himmel is gathered in the Great Hall. We take a quick head count and I could tell even before it was concluded that we were much smaller. The room does not fill the way it should.

There are still 384 Royals here in Roter Himmel. That includes Malachi and Dorian. That includes Mina, Fredrick, Horatio. It includes me and Cyrus.

Outside our borders, the army, who number six thousand, keep Lorenzo and the betrayers out of the city.

There are 308 of Lorenzo's children either here, or soon to arrive. Thirty-two Royals walked away from us. Others could rally and join them.

352 vampires on the side of the Crown.

340 vampires on Lorenzo's side.

Shit.

I really, really don't like those numbers.

Everyone sits or stands, gathered around Cyrus and I in the center of the room. Ideas and problems are shouted out, both by the crowd and by Cyrus and myself. Anyone who has anything to say is free to speak.

First and most important: has anyone seen Lorenzo since his escape a few hours ago?

No.

Has anyone seen signs of his four children that were here in Court?

No.

"We must rally the Houses," Mina says loudly. "The numbers will skew in our favor with all of them at our side."

"And just leave the rest of the world to go mad?" Dorian counters her. "If you pull every one of the Royals to Roter Himmel, it won't take more than a few days for the rest of the Born in the world to realize they're unchecked."

"Is this not why the Crown takes such good care of the Houses?" Mina says loudly. "The Houses were handed to them, maintained financially, backed, so that when the time came, when the Crown needs them, they will stand at our side."

"Who is to say that every House will side with Cyrus and Sevan?" a man I do not know speaks up. "Who is to say that some of them won't side with Lorenzo?"

"Because of the exact reasons I just stated," Mina says, frustration rising in her voice. "No, not everyone may be enamored with the King, but he has taken care of them in every way for centuries or millennia. They would be ungrateful fools to turn against him in this hour of need."

The crowd falls silent for a moment, considering that.

I really don't know what to expect in that regard. Yes, it's true that Cyrus has taken care of the Houses all this time. But how many of them would truly be loyal to him in a war? How many would come to Cyrus' aid?

If they turn against us and Lorenzo wins, the system of the Houses will most likely crumble and they will lose everything.

But how many around the world are truly happy living in secret?

"The issue of the Houses is a matter for Sevan and I to decide upon," Cyrus says loudly, his voice carrying through the large space without effort. "For now, we need to arm ourselves. We need to prepare for the kind of war we have not fought in a millennia and a half."

I look around and I wonder: how many of them were there when we fought the war against my son? There was Dorian and Malachi, fighting by my side. But is there anyone else left? Have any of the others survived all these years?

It seems impossible.

I wonder now how my grandsons have survived this long.

"We need spies," Cyrus says. "This may be a lack of foresight on my part, that I have not replaced my head spy since the dismissal of Raheem." There's thickness in his voice at the mention of his name. And I can tell, it is difficult for him still, to be betrayed like he was by his most trusted spy in all of his history. "But I know there are others here who are incredibly capable. Gunter, Resseme, and Brynn."

Each of the three steps forward, standing in a line before us. "The safety of Roter Himmel depends on you in these next critical days. I need you and others you deem capable to keep an eye on the happenings in the mountains."

Every one of them nods and without a word, heads toward the doors. They tap others on the shoulder as they walk by, and in all, nine individuals walk out the doors to go spy on Lorenzo.

"If all of Lorenzo's children haven't yet arrived," Malachi speaks up, "our best chance is to attack now. We may still outnumber them. Better we attack before they rally, slaughter them with the numbers fewer."

"And then take care of the rest as they arrive," Cyrus concludes. I see his eyes alight brilliant red. A spark of excitement makes them brilliant. "We will wait two hours for a full report from our spies. But be prepared." He lifts his chin, and I remember that look in his eyes from before. I remember the danger there. When we went into a war that lasted seven years. "Arm yourselves for battle."

A great cry echoes through the Great Hall and the entire population springs to action.

They know where the armories within the castle are. Most of them, anyway. They flood out from the Hall to arm themselves, prepared to strike at a word from their King.

I leave to prepare for war, too, heading straight for the stairs. Cyrus follows, matching me step for step.

I change into fighting leathers, secure boots with straps and buckles. Cyrus dresses similarly, his battered and scarred crown resting upon his head.

We arm ourselves from our private armory with stakes and guns, grenades and gas bombs.

From a safe buried in the wall, we unearth two swords—the very same swords we wielded in the war against our son. The one Cyrus used when he cut our son's head from his body.

Armed to the teeth, we rejoin the others.

In our very long lives, it seems like two hours should go by quickly. But it's as if each minute is an hour. Quietly we wait, our eyes trained on the mouth of the canyon.

Just hours ago, as the human army marched toward the canyon, Lorenzo's children retreated. Now, as we look toward the mountains, all I can see is Matthias' army.

The first hour passes.

I think of the last war we fought here on Roter Himmel's soil.

Another thirty minutes go by.

I remember the lives we lost the first time we fought for our secrecy.

Another ten minutes goes by.

And then through the dark, we see the shape of three figures headed up the road toward us.

Gunter, Brynn, and Matthias.

I step forward, followed by Cyrus, to meet them half way in the middle of the road.

"They're smarter than I would have hoped for," Gunter speaks first. "We searched the canyon, went all the way back to the town, even back into the next one. There were no signs of Lorenzo's descendants."

"Any of them?" I question, sure I'm misunderstanding him. "Any of the dozens and dozens?"

"None of them, Sevan."

"Well, where the hell did they go?" I demand, my brows furrowing.

"I did find one group, hiding in the woods," Brynn says. As I look at her, I realize she's covered in splashes of blood. "They were hiding."

"They split off," Matthias jumps in. "About three hours ago, they started splitting off into groups, heading back away from Roter Himmel. They were…discrete about it. It took us a while to realize what they were doing."

"So now they're spread out, who knows where, just… watching us?" I ask in horror.

"And you and your army did nothing to stop them?" Cyrus seethes. His eyes glow brilliant in the darkness, and the wrath on his face makes him look terrifying.

"Our army came to help contain four hundred individuals who were not expecting our arrival," Matthias says. And I am impressed. He stands up to both Cyrus and I without hesitation. "That, up there, was a bomb waiting to detonate. That, up there, was *far* more than a hundred individuals, and I will not take unnecessary risks with the lives I am in charge of."

I feel my face go cold. "More than a hundred," I say. "How many are there now?"

"At least double that," Matthias says, snapping his eyes to me.

Two hundred. With more arriving every minute.

And now, those already here are hiding.

Without another word, Cyrus turns and goes back to the crowd at the castle gates. I follow him wordlessly.

"I want hunting parties," Cyrus says. "Groups. I want you to form teams of ten. Three hunting parties are to go out at one time. We will scour the woods and mountains that surround us. And we will slaughter any descendants we come upon."

There's instant talking, instant movement. Without having to be overseen, they automatically begin forming groups, ten each, as Cyrus instructed. This makes thirty-five groups.

I understand why Cyrus doesn't send them all at once. We have to be careful we do not get ambushed. And we can't leave the castle unprotected.

"Go," Cyrus says, indicating the first three groups standing at the forefront of the crowd. Without hesitating, they head out, darting toward the mountains at lightning speeds.

"This is insanity," Cyrus says quietly under his breath. "Someone so small, so insignificant for such a long time, should not be this much of a problem."

I reach over and take Cyrus' hand in mine. "We will end this," I promise. Not just to him, but to myself.

CHAPTER 5

"And that takes the total up to what?" Cyrus asks.

Brynn shifts uncomfortably under the weight of the King's eyes, standing beside Matthias. "Twelve," she reports.

Twelve. Twelve is the tiny number we have found and slaughtered of the descendants in the last three days we have been hunting for them.

We've been hunting the surrounding mountains. We've searched the nearest villages. Every square meter within a hundred miles surrounding Roter Himmel has been searched and re-searched.

And twelve is the grand total number of descendants we've found.

"What if they've left?" Matthias suggests. "Perhaps Lorenzo realized he was outnumbered with my army taken into consideration. Maybe he realized how futile this was. Maybe he took his children and retreated."

"I wish that were the case," I say as I lean against the

edge of Cyrus' desk, folding my arms over my chest. "But Lorenzo was patient for six hundred years. He managed to wait all that time for all those children to be born. I just can't imagine now that we know, now that he's exposed them all, and told us the truth, that he will just squander this opportunity. It's now or never, I think."

"He must be waiting for something," Cyrus says. He sits in his chair, his booted feet propped up on his desk. "Perhaps not all of his children have arrived yet. Perhaps he has retreated to make plans. Perhaps they are even gathering at a location where they have been stockpiling weapons."

"There's any number of reasons why he isn't striking yet," I conclude, nodding in agreement with Cyrus. "But we can't let our defenses down. If Roter Himmel is taken, we'll fall. This is our stronghold. This is the center of everything. If we lose Roter Himmel, we'll lose the war. Continue to hold the borders."

Matthias and Brynn both give a bow, and leave the office.

"I don't like this kind of warfare," Cyrus says. He twirls the sword between his fingers, the point of it spinning on the ground, the hilt held loosely in his fingers. "All this waiting and hiding. If Lorenzo St. Claire wants to take my crown, he should just march to the doors and rip it from my head."

"He thinks differently than us," I say. "I can't imagine the patience the man must possess. He's waited six centuries to make his move."

Cyrus is quiet for a moment, and finally, his eyes slide over to me. "I don't even remember it, you know?" He studies me a moment longer, but I know it isn't me he's really seeing. "Lorenzo said I killed his parents because they were caught drinking from a human. But I don't remember it. I don't remember his father's name. I don't remember his mother trying to save him. I don't remember a young boy having to watch it happen."

His gaze slides over to a wall and they glaze over. I can feel the weight upon his shoulders filling the room. I feel it press down on me, too.

I walk around the desk. I push his feet off its polished surface and straddle his hips, sitting in his lap.

But his gaze is still fixed on the wall, not seeing anything.

"It is no wonder he hates me so much," Cyrus continues to muse. "I ripped his family away, and don't even remember doing it. He thinks me a monster who doesn't value family, and now he wishes to take them all and make them one."

I place my hands on either side of Cyrus' face, attempting to turn his gaze to me. It takes a moment, but finally he does look at me with his sad, weighted eyes.

"You are not a monster," I say. "You are only cruel to protect our people. You do the things you must to keep us safe. They may not recognize it and that is because they have never had to live in fear. But you know, and I know, the life that would await us if we were exposed. Lorenzo's father knew he should have been more careful. He knew the potential consequences for doing what he did. You have to enforce the rules to protect us all."

There's pain in Cyrus' eyes. There's regret. He squeezes them closed, and I press my forehead to his, wrapping my arms around his shoulders, holding him close.

"I'm so tired of it all, Sevan," he says quietly. "I'm tired of the games. I'm tired of the politics. I'm tired of ruling."

Emotion bites the back of my eyes, but I don't let the tears well. My heart does twist in a knot, though. My stomach feels so heavy. "I know, *im yndmisht srtov*. Me, too."

THE NEXT NIGHT, AT TWO IN THE MORNING, GUNTER BURSTS through the doors of the Great Hall, where Cyrus and I were meeting with Dorian and Malachi. He's breathing hard, a heavy sweat on his brow.

"They've returned," he says, his eyes jumping from one face to another. "They're in the village just through the canyon."

"How many of them?" I ask.

"I'd say around three hundred of them," he says.

All of them.

"I want to see them," I say, grabbing the sword laying on the table and slinging it around my waist. "Take me to them."

Cyrus is instantly on his feet as well, followed by Dorian and Malachi. "Stay," Cyrus growls at them. "I need you two to be here in case anything happens."

Without another backward glance, Cyrus and I follow Gunter.

We're more silent on foot than in a vehicle. We're less noticeable creeping through the woods than in the helicopter. So, across the valley we dart, cutting around the stationed army. Through the canyon, off the road in the trees we race.

Gunter leads us along a mountain ridge, and off in the distance, I can see dim, glowing lights.

We round the ridge, and a rocky outcropping juts through

the trees, providing the perfect overlook of the smaller valley. The village so tiny I can hardly call it that. It consists only of an inn, a gas station, a postal office, and the airport. There are only a dozen homes here, and every one of those occupants is employed in the businesses they're surrounded by.

My eyes widen. My heart wants to stop.

There are so many bodies down below. Not one hundred, not two. There has to be at least three hundred of them down there.

They mill about the street, the main one that cuts through the heart of the village. They wander in and out of the homes, the businesses.

I see a human woman down there, limp and slack in a man's arms as he drinks her blood. He passes her onto a woman, who drinks deeply. From the paleness of the human woman's skin, I know there won't be any recovering from how much they've taken.

As I look around, I realize there is more than one human being passed around. I can see five others from here.

I can only imagine the others are dead already.

They've taken over the entire village, and wiped out the human population.

"Any eyes on Lorenzo?" I whisper, barely audible to even my own ears.

Gunter shakes his head. "We have our best snipers watching the area. They all know what he looks like. At the first sight of him, they've been ordered to take him out."

My eyes search the crowd, looking for any signs of the man with the dark hair and features, and golden-jade eyes.

He's nowhere to be seen. But as I search, looking over all those half-siblings of mine, I realize something.

"That has to be more than three hundred individuals down there," I say. "Doesn't...doesn't that look like more than three hundred?"

The two of them are quiet for a good thirty seconds as they try to mentally calculate.

While I wait for their conclusion, my eyes whip to the right when a flash of light drops from the sky.

A plane dips toward the airport that isn't visible from this vantage point.

No one travels into this airport unless they're somehow connected to Roter Himmel.

"You're right," Cyrus says. "My rough estimate is closer to 380."

I look back at the crowd, and my blood feels cold. "Lorenzo told me he has 308 children from around the world. We've killed twelve of them already. There's the thirty-two Royals who betrayed us. But who...who are the others?"

More lights above us draw my eyes up. I see another airplane circling the valley, beginning its descent.

"Who the hell is coming?" I hiss. My heart is pounding and my brain is screaming a million miles an hour.

"Perhaps Lorenzo lied about how many children he has," Gunter suggests.

My nerves are strung out. I'm ready to snap at any moment. And hopefully when I blow, I take every one of them out with me.

"Come on," I say quietly as I slink back into the trees. "We need to see what's going on at that airport."

We're incredibly careful. We slip behind trees. We melt into the shadows of the night. I take to the branches. I don't even breathe as we slip around the town's edges and head to the outskirts where the airport is located.

The three of us take position beside a hangar, silently slipping along the edge of the metal building, until the airstrip comes into view.

The three jets are taxied, side by side. And there, at the base of them, a good two hundred yards away, I see a crowd.

There are twenty-one individuals gathered together, talking in low voices.

"Do either of you recognize any of them?" I whisper.

Cyrus and Gunter both shake their heads.

Falling silent, we each strain our eyes, trying to pick up on the voices.

"...has been able to speak with their leader," one voice faintly floats to my ears. "They won't even say his name. But they all stem from the same father, obvious by their looks. It has to be him."

"Are they causing any problems for us?" another sounds across the runway.

There's a muffle I can't quite interpret. "So far, they only have questions about our intent."

There's laughing, and it makes my skin crawl.

"From what little we've overheard, their goal is the same as ours."

All of my internal organs disappear with the words. Automatically, my eyes flick to Cyrus, who looks at me with similar wide, but ready to fight eyes.

Word spread far and wide of King Cyrus' death. And with it, all the greedy tyrants came out to play.

We not only have Lorenzo to worry about, but whoever these people are, as well.

The meeting seemingly over, the group before us heads toward the road that cuts into the village.

With a dark look at one another, Cyrus turns to Gunter.

"The stakes were just raised ten fold," Cyrus breathes. "Double the amount of spies. Collect every word spoken in that village. I want hourly reports."

"Yes, your majesty," he responds with a deep bow.

Not another word, Cyrus and I streak like lightning back to the castle.

CHAPTER 6

I STALK THROUGH THE DOORS TO CYRUS' OFFICE AND FLING the first thing my hands find across the room. The glass jar filled with teeth shatters against the far wall.

Teeth. From all the liars who have crossed Cyrus' path over the centuries.

"This is insane," I hiss. "This is so damn insane and it just keeps getting worse and worse!"

I seethe, placing my hands on Cyrus' desk, glowering at its polished surface.

I'm overflowing with anger. With kinetic, destructive energy. I could burn down all the forests that surround me with the heat washing over me.

I look to the side and see Cyrus close the doors behind him. He studies me with those intense eyes as he leans back against the door.

And suddenly, I need an outlet. I need to pour some acid out of me.

Cyrus knows what's coming. I can see it in his eyes as I stalk across the room. I see his body tense and prepare for it. I see the hunger and excitement alight in his eyes as I close the distance between us.

My hands instantly tangle into his hair and I roughly pull his face to mine. Cyrus' lips aren't gentle when they connect with mine, and I don't hesitate in taking his lower lip between my teeth.

His hands go to my hips and I just don't have any kind of patience right now. I climb him, assisted as his hands clamp onto my ass and he lifts me. My legs wrap around his waist, pressing myself against him tightly.

A needy, greedy grunt works its way out of my chest, over my lips. I wrap my arms behind his neck, shifting my kisses from his lips to his neck, nipping and sucking as I work my way across his skin.

Cyrus carries me across the office. With a sweep of his arm across his desk, he clears everything from it and lays me on my back across it.

Even better.

He can press himself all the harder into my center now.

We're both angry right now. We're both filled to the brim with revenge and spite. And we're taking it out on one another's bodies.

And it's everything.

My hands dig into Cyrus' shirt, and a moment later, it shreds to pieces. I smile as he meets my eyes for a moment, and I let the pieces fall to the floor.

Cyrus lifts the hem of my own shirt and I let my head fall

back and my eyes slide closed as his lips come to my stomach.

"Cyrus," I moan as he works his way up, pushing the fabric further up my torso as he climbs higher.

"Say it again, Logan," he growls against my skin.

I fist my fingers in his hair, making sure he can't escape. "I want you, Cyrus," I pant. In one quick movement, he splits my shirt, ripping it clean in half. He flings the fabric across the room. "I never wanted anyone else in my entire life. Because every other man was too boring. To calm. To clean."

Cyrus kisses his way over my bra, up between my breasts. His hand comes to one side of my throat as he licks his way up the other side of it.

"I want a king who can burn down the entire damn world," I breathe, hardly able to speak through the raging desire inside of me. "I want you, Cyrus." My hands travel south, reaching for the belt around his waist. Greedily, I pull at it, unlatching the leather. "I want you, now."

"I will take you, Logan," Cyrus growls against my skin. I feel his fangs lengthen, and a small prick as they pierce my skin. He climbs up on top of the desk, sliding me forward to make room.

Nearly falling off the edge, I throw out a hand to brace myself, all reason in me gone, replaced entirely by need and desire, when my hand falls to the chair at the desk. And it meets something sharp, and something else wet...and hairy.

Annoyed at the distraction, my eyes momentarily dart to the chair, even as Cyrus undoes my own belt and the button of my pants.

But a scream erupts from my lungs, over my lips.

My hand is smeared with blood.

And sitting on the chair is Cyrus' crown. And carefully placed in the center of it, is a bloody scalp of snow-white hair.

I know whose it is immediately. Only one member of Court has hair that void of color.

Fredrick.

Confused, Cyrus rises onto his hands, and the moment his eyes meet the scalp bloodying his chair, his face pales.

"Moab," he breathes.

My lungs are swallowed up by the roiling pit of acid that is my stomach.

Cyrus pulls me to my feet and I walk around the desk, staring down at the white hair on the chair.

I shake my head. I try to speak, but the words get caught in my throat. I swallow once. But my mouth is too dry.

I'm flung back in time, falling through nearly twenty centuries.

"He's still alive?" I finally manage to speak.

Cyrus reaches forward as if he's going to grab the scalp of his assistant, but seems to think better of it, instead, crossing his arms over his chest.

"Do you remember?" he asks, "when we interrogated a man over some peculiar deaths? When you wore Edith's face?"

I nod as I fight the urge to vomit. I do remember. I remember it very specifically as Cyrus interrogated and tortured the man.

"He implied Moab had escaped. That what had happened during that time was him."

I search my memory for what came after that. But all I can find is darkness.

I know what that means.

It means I died another death shortly after the memory.

"I went to the tomb and confirmed myself," Cyrus says. "He'd somehow escaped and has been missing for the past 367 years."

"How?" I breathe. My mind is tracing a path mentally, going through tunnels and secret passages through the castle.

Down into the dark.

Down into the heart of the mountain.

"I still do not know," Cyrus confesses.

Long ago, long, long ago, Cyrus and I had a son. After he Resurrected, after he forsook us and turned his back against every one of our fears, he went out into the world. And his mission was to create others like him.

He succeeded.

He conceived and different mothers bore him seven sons and thirteen daughters.

In the end it came to the great war. A division split. Those who stood with us, who knew we had to remain hidden, in secret, if we did not wish to be eliminated. And then there were those who sided with our son. Who wanted to take over the world.

Only two of our grandsons sided with Cyrus and I. Dorian and Malachi, the third and seventh sons.

Five sided with their father.

Two were killed.

Two were banished. They left Roter Himmel in shame, and were killed only years later by some of the loyal.

But the other, the first born to our son, Moab—Cyrus never let him escape.

Deep in the castle, down a tunnel that allows not a sliver of light, located behind a locked gate, there is a lightless room.

In the floor, there is a tomb.

It is hewn from the granite of the mountain, a hole only three feet deep and six feet long. There is a boulder that rests over the top of it, so many thousands of pounds that it takes six vampires to move it, inch by inch.

When the war was over, when our son was dead, and the disloyal disowned and chased off, Cyrus took his firstborn grandson, and with his most trusted soldiers, he laid Moab in the tomb and closed it up.

For over sixteen centuries Moab had been trapped in the belly of the mountain.

Vampires are immortal. They cannot die without a stake through the heart, or a beheading—save Cyrus. So he lay in the ground for centuries, starving and withering into desiccation.

But somehow, when I was Edith, Moab escaped.

Moab was the most devoted to his father of all my son's children. The first born, all he wished for was to help his father rise to power and fame. He worshiped his father.

It was in his very name.

Moab—Hebrew for *of his father*.

In life, in the horror leading up to the war, Moab had his signature kill proof.

The beheading and scalping of any vampires who stood in his way.

"It seems we have not one enemy to wipe from the face of the earth," Cyrus says solemnly, "but two."

CHAPTER 7

FREDRICK'S BODY IS FOUND DISCARDED DOWN BY THE LAKE.
His head is nowhere to be found. The guards go into lock-down mode, searching for any signs of Moab or how he, or one of his spies, entered the castle.

None are found.

Within twenty-four hours, there are another hundred Born outside the city. Our spies report there still have been no signs of Lorenzo, or Moab. Wherever they are, they're hiding well. They're being careful.

And one week since this all started, the world goes to a new level of insanity.

"Come again?" Cyrus says, raising an eyebrow at Brynn.

"They're all fighting," she says. "So far there are only a few that have actually been killed, but there's definitely a rift. A division. Lorenzo's children and those who rallied with Moab, they don't exactly seem to like each other."

Neither of us can believe it. So together, Cyrus and I once

more carefully sneak our way to the settlement, watching from our lookout point.

She was right. Down below, the masses argue in the streets. Fists fly. Guns and swords are drawn.

I can physically see a split happening. It's easy to pick out Lorenzo's children. They all have the same eyes as me, that same bright, golden-jade. Apparently, it's a heavily dominant trait. And the others, they are pushed to the edges of the small town. They take up residence on the airport side.

It's advantageous. They continue to have more Born arriving almost hourly.

Not daring to speak here where we may be overheard, where there are likely scouts and spies circling their encampment, Cyrus and I head back to Roter Himmel.

"There can only be one reason why they're waiting to attack," I say as we walk up the road back to the castle. "They know they're outnumbered right now with Matthias' army. They're waiting for more reinforcements to arrive."

We step through the castle gates and head back toward Cyrus' office.

"The time has arrived," Cyrus says. "We must strike now. We must put this to bed before they grow stronger. We will attack in one hour."

Stepping through the doors, we both falter, finding four individuals inside, waiting for us.

Dorian, Malachi, Mina, and Matthias.

Gravely, they look at us, and my heart instantly sinks.

"What is it?" Cyrus demands, his expression full of dread.

Matthias steps forward, his face grave and fallen. "My soldiers are sick."

"Sick?" I repeat. "Like, they've all got colds or something?"

Slowly, Matthias' expression shifts into anger. "No, as in they've been poisoned. The water supply to this town comes from that canyon, from a lake up above where that mutiny is forming. I'm saying that us humans are dependent on water. And while none of you vampires might have even noticed that there's something wrong with the water, we humans have been drinking it, and now we have failing livers and kidneys. We are literally dying out there."

I feel my face blanch. My fingers feel cold. "How many of them have been affected?"

Matthias steps forward, eye to eye with me, his hands on his hips. I didn't notice the sweat on his brow until now, the bloodshot look in his eyes. "Every single one of us, to some degree. Some are still standing, at least. Aren't puking their guts up. But seventy percent can't even walk right now."

I swear.

Looking over at Cyrus, my eyes widen, and I know he's thinking what I am: how did we not anticipate this? Those humans were our greatest defense because of their numbers. They were our back up. Our safety net.

And I didn't even once think to protect them.

"I'm so sorry," I breathe, looking back at Matthias. "I..."

"You should take a good look at yourself, Queen Sevan," Matthias spits. "You say you're fighting this war to protect the humans, to keep the world from being destroyed. But are you really that different from Lorenzo? From Moab? Do you really care about the human population that founded this earth? Because right now, your actions speak louder than your words."

With a disgusted look on his face, he turns and heads toward the doors. He pauses there, and looks back at Dorian and Malachi. "Our deal is done," he says gravely. "If I can, I'm taking my men and we're leaving. Don't come calling again."

My stomach sinks all the further.

Dorian and Malachi called in huge favors to help me. They did this because I asked them to.

And now they've both lost major allies.

"I don't know what you're waiting for," Mina speaks through the weighted silence at Matthias' departure. "There is a very quick, very easy way to end this."

All remaining eyes flick to her.

"Roter Himmel may be old in most ways," she says, fishing into her pocket. She produces something that looks like a small remote control. "But we have certainly kept up on modern weaponry."

I know what she's holding now. It's a detonator for a bomb.

"You drop it over the center of that encampment," she says, twirling it between her fingers. "You take every one of them out all at once. No lives even lost."

"Do you know what bombs do, Mina?" Cyrus asks, fixing her with a cold, hard stare.

This is a woman who has served her king for some time. I can tell when her eyes drop and she shifts half a step back from him.

Cyrus suddenly darts forward, snatching the detonator from her fingers with one hand, and fisting his hand in her jacket with the other. He shoves her back, smacking her head against the wall.

"They make noise," Cyrus says. "They shake the ground. They set off Richter scales." His face is in hers, seething through his teeth. "They draw a lot of attention."

"Cyrus," I snap. My fingers curl into fists. "That's enough."

Instantly, he releases her. Mina tries to hold her expression steady, but I see in her eyes, the fear and the shock. She straightens her jacket, and awkwardly, without a word, she turns and leaves the office.

"She was only trying to help," I chide Cyrus.

Cyrus lets out a long breath through his nostrils as he turns from me, facing the map that spreads out on the wall. But he does not apologize.

I follow his line of sight. It's a map of the entire world. And marked with small knives buried into the wall behind the map, are all the Houses.

"We cannot rely on the human army now," Malachi says. I'd forgotten my grandsons were still in the room. "We're outnumbered by far without them."

"I'm afraid it's time," Dorian chimes in. "We need to call on the Houses for aid."

I step forward, picking up the phone resting on Cyrus' desk. I consider for a moment.

Who first?

Who do I drag into this mess?

Who do I dare risk in this war?

I'm a terrible person. Because the first House I call isn't the House of Marshalls. It isn't the House of Conrath.

After five rings, the line connects.

"How may I be of service?" Edmond Valdez' voice comes through from across the world.

WHEN WE SHOULD BE MARCHING ACROSS THE VALLEY, through the canyon, and slaughtering the mutiny army, we're on the phone, making dozens of calls.

It takes us more than five hours to get in touch with every single House in the world. With all four of us making the phone calls.

In the end, I let Dorian make the call to the House of Conrath and Cyrus calls the House of Marshalls.

We explain everything. The situation with Lorenzo. The legend of Moab and his dedication to the Blood Father. How they've rallied and are preparing to attack at any moment.

We ask for them to come. To help defend Roter Himmel.

We ask them to make a stand for their way of life.

We're met with hesitation. While they all live comfortable lives because the Crown supports them, we're asking them to uproot their lives and come join a war. A *war*. Most of them have never had to fight a war. Sure, they've all settled small skirmishes, or fought small battles to keep their region in check.

But this *will* be a war.

They know what will happen if they do not come to the aid of the crown.

Cyrus will strip them of their titles. He'll exile them. They'll never hold the title of Royal again.

That is, if we come out on top of this the victors.

I hang up from my last phone call, to the House in Brazil.

I look over at Cyrus, and then Dorian and Malachi.

I have no idea what to expect. With our phone calls, the entire world now knows that our way of life is in upheaval. That there's a revolution attempting to start. Now they all have the idea planted in their heads that maybe there is another way, different from the way it's been done for thousands of years.

In the end, we may have just hurried along our demise.

Why are you fighting this battle? a little voice asks in the back of my brain. *No matter what, things will never be the same. Your world is forever changed. Why are you fighting? What are you fighting for?*

My jaw hardens as I look at the map of the Houses.

I'm fighting because I'm not a damn coward. I won't go running.

I'm fighting because this is the world I helped create. This is what I worked tirelessly for in creating Roter Himmel.

I'll fight for peace. I'll fight for safety. I'll fight for my family.

I FEEL THIS TICKING IN THE BACK OF MY BRAIN. EVERY single second feels critical. We're just waiting here, sitting ducks. Every second we wait, the forces outside our borders grow bigger and stronger.

The last count we received was 509 total Born and Royal outside the borders.

Here we sit with only 352 of us.

There are only 108 more Royals in the entire world.

Even if every one of them comes, we are still outnumbered.

Some of them will bring their Born House members with them to fight. But we can't count on that. Because they are Born. And this is a war to change the division between the Born and the Royals.

Even more than the desire to come out of hiding, to go into the public light, that will be our downfall. That we have oppressed the Born for all this time. That they are less-than in this world we created.

That will be what ends us.

We make arrangements for travelers. With the Born and Lorenzo's children having overrun our airport, we're forced to make arrangements with another, which is an hour away. We have two helicopters here at the castle. Our pilots make non-stop runs back and forth transporting the arriving Royals.

Those close by arrive within hours of our phone calls. The House of Badillo, O'Rorque, and Emile are the first to arrive. Located closely in Spain, Scotland, and France, they add fifteen to our numbers.

One of the most experienced in warfare, the House of Badillo, from Spain, takes over making sure that our numbers are armed at all times. They begin battle regimens. Training.

I can hardly breathe. I keep looking out the windows, waiting to see a flood of half-siblings and Born wash down into the valley. They could strike at any moment. My hands hardly leave the sword slung at my side.

Just as evening begins to descend, one of Dorian's Houses in Russia arrives, soon followed by Malachi's in Egypt.

With the castle getting fuller by the moment, I go to Cyrus' office and stare at the map on the wall.

Who hasn't arrived that should have?

The House in Brazil could have been here by now. The House of Nnamani in Guinea, Africa could have been here.

I try not to think about what that means. If it means they just aren't coming. If it means they're really here, but joining Lorenzo or Moab. Or if it really is just taking some time to arrive.

I can't do anything to change that right now. The damage that might turn them against us was done long, long ago.

But right now, there is something I can do.

There is one place help is needed and I can grant it.

Leaving the office, I head down a hall. Spotting Mina, I call to her and she turns to me, waiting for orders.

"I need your help," I simply say. "Go find four others who can be spared and meet me in the garage."

She's gone in an instant.

Five minutes later, the six of us sweep through the garage, evaluating the vehicles available to us.

We have four trucks and a Hummer.

None of us say much. Mina climbs into the Hummer with me, and carefully, we spiral our way down through the tunnel that climbs out of the belly of the castle. We're spit out into the dark, on a quiet side road. We aim for the encampment only a mile from the mouth of the canyon.

My stomach is roiling with guilt as we drive out across the valley.

I'm taking a risk by coming out here, but I put that army in this situation. I have to do what I can to help.

Throughout this entire day, Matthias has been moving his army out of the valley. They're taking a treacherous route over the mountain, through a narrow valley, into a town thirty minutes away with a small hospital.

As we roll up to the camp, I take a mental count. There were once 6,000 soldiers here. Now before me, I see a meager few hundred.

They're dying, but they've been taking care of themselves.

We park the vehicle close to the tents and I climb out.

I see Matthias, another man's arm slung over his shoulders. He eyes me warily as he helps the man over to a vehicle, putting him in the backseat. All of his body language screams trepidation as he walks over to me.

"We're here to help," I say.

Inside, I'm screaming. Because I don't have time to do this. At any second our world could be ripped apart as the battle begins.

But I have to make this right. Or Matthias will be right. I'll be no better than Lorenzo or Moab.

Matthias only nods once and points in the direction of the sick soldiers.

I tell him we need to pick up the pace, that we must transport as many soldiers as we can with each load. So when we set off over the mountain the first time, every vehicle has at least ten soldiers crammed in it. The army had dozens of their own vehicles, and every able-bodied soldier has been doing transport.

I assist for six hours. Carrying men from their cots, some of them smelling like vomit. Some of them so pale white their skin is nearly translucent. I put them in vehicles. And then I drive precariously over the mountain and through the pass.

We arrive at the overwhelmed hospital bearing more and more men and women. They're already transporting them to another three hospitals, just trying to keep up.

We're being exposed already.

The doctors have questions.

The local authorities have questions.

And we don't have answers.

In all, I make six round trips before I help load the last twenty men into the vehicles. But another vehicle comes bouncing over the terrain and parks just a few yards away.

Out of the vehicle, steps Edmond Valdez.

"The King needs you," he says, eying the strange scene before him.

I nod and then turn, catching Matthias' eye. Wiping my hands on my pants, I cross the distance between us. "The others will stay," I say. "They'll help until the job is done."

He nods, and I can see there are words on the tip of his tongue that he just can't quite say.

"You did what I asked you to come here and do," I say. "I know it evolved into something none of us expected, but without you and your soldiers, the chaos would have come more quickly. There would have been more bloodshed. The ripples would have been felt throughout the world a lot faster."

He looks over at me, but only for a moment. He still can't find his words.

"We're really trying, you know," I say. "All of this, it's for your kind. We're trying to keep ourselves under wraps. I know it got a lot more intense than it should have. But I don't want you walking out of here filled with resentment. I don't want you to hate me."

Matthias' eyes flick to mine. "I don't hate you, Sevan," he says. He straightens, folding his arms across his chest. "I think all of this has gotten too much for you to handle, for Cyrus to handle. I think it's a miracle you've kept all of this so steady and level for as long as you have. The times are shifting and changing, and I don't know what's going to come. But I don't hate you, Sevan. I think in a bizarre way, I admire you."

The weight on my chest gets just a little lighter at his granted words. I offer him a small smile, and extend a hand.

He takes it, shaking mine.

"Thank you for everything you've done," I say.

"Good luck," he offers, and I can tell he means it, but is doubtful.

I'm doubtful, too. But I turn, and walk back to Edmond and his vehicle. Together, we drive back to the castle.

CHAPTER 8

I TWIST MY HAIR BACK IN AN ELEGANT KNOT. I CAN'T FIND A smile anywhere on my lips as I carefully set my crown upon my head. A knot of dread is in my stomach as I lace up my gown.

I'm done. *I'm done.*

I'm so done.

The words echo through my head as I numbly try not to think about everything.

Walk away.

Leave it all behind.

Cyrus was right.

He was right.

But I fought for this.

I didn't know all the details of what was going on, or what was to come, but I fought for this. Now I have to see it through to the end.

But I'm just so tired.

Feeling empty and depleted, I step out of the bathroom and find Cyrus waiting there for me.

He must see the heaviness in my eyes, in my expression. He pulls me into his chest and wraps his arms around me, cradling my head against him.

He doesn't say anything, and I think he's feeling the same things I am.

Is it worth it anymore?

What are we still fighting for?

But I don't have time to sit and wallow. Cyrus doesn't have time. Our world doesn't have time.

I straighten. I brush Cyrus' jacket flat again. I take his hand and I walk through the halls with him, side by side.

The volume of the voices spilling from the Great Hall is nearly enough to rumble the castle floors. I take one more pause, one more moment, surrendering myself to Queen Sevan, before the both of us step inside.

There are so many here. There are roughly three hundred fifty court members. More than forty of us are out scouting and spying. And then there are around two dozen familiar and non-familiar faces, Royals who came to our aide.

The House of Valdez, with Hector and Edmond.

I remember the members of the House of Himura, who I was last a descendant of.

The leaders of the House of Cordero are the same.

There are many faces I don't recognize. Leadership has changed in the 286 years I was dead or missing.

But they're here.

Many are not.

The room is set up with four long tables, another set up at the head of the room. Every Royal sits along the tables, the room packed and full.

I walk by Cyrus' side, and every eye is fixed on us as we go to the head table.

Neither of us speaks for a long moment. We both stare out, looking back at our descendants that surround us.

I take note. Alivia has not yet arrived.

A wicked voice in the back of my head whispers doubt. States that there is the possibility that she isn't coming.

I tell myself I don't care if she does.

But it's a lie.

"Brothers and sisters," Cyrus says. His voice cuts through the massive space with clarity and evenness. "Sons and daughters. Sevan and I welcome you to Court and give you our deepest depths of gratitude for coming."

Cyrus holds my hand, and I note all the eyes that watch us. There are small smiles. Softness in certain eyes.

I know the legends we bring with us. I know that they know the stories of my death, occurring over and over. For 286 years they've known the Queen was dead.

And here I am. Here we are, Cyrus and I, together.

"For a very long time we have lived in relatively consistent peace," Cyrus continues. "There have been issues, small instances to be dealt with. But we have remained safe. We have stayed out of the spotlight. We have kept to ourselves."

The room is absolutely silent. They listen on baited breath. They wait for reassurances as to why they're here.

"Throughout the years there have been many who questioned why we should hide who and what we are," Cyrus continues, his voice increasing slightly in volume. "Individuals have contested why we must live in fear, when we are so much stronger than those we once were."

A memory flashes through my head. Of the two of us running through the dark. Of an angry mob chasing after us with torches and pitchforks and swords. I recall placing a rag between my teeth, trying to stifle my screams in the dark so that I didn't expose us.

"A long, long time ago," Cyrus says, and I know exactly where he's headed in this moment, "I was the lone and sole vampire in this world. It was terrifying adjusting to and learning about the bloodlust that seemed to transform me into a different person. And I exposed myself. I exposed my family."

Cyrus squeezes my hand, an apology expressed a million times over the thousands of years. I squeeze it back, a reassurance that he was forgiven a long, long time ago.

"Sevan and I were forced to move," Cyrus says. "When she became what I am, when there were two of us who needed their blood, we no longer had a home."

I let my eyes slide closed, remembering that fear.

"When others realized what we were doing, they wanted to kill us," Cyrus presses on. "They wanted to torture us. They tried. So we had no choice but to run, because even though we were so much stronger than them, there were only two of us, and there were thousands of them."

Thump. *Thump thump.*

My heart rate increases with the fear, the recollection of those times.

"We were chased from our home country," Cyrus says. "We had to flee hundreds of miles away. And then we found this place." Cyrus' voice cuts out, and the room is silent for five heartbeats. "Roter Himmel. Red Heaven. We were alone, we were isolated for dozens of years. But we finally found peace. We found a place where we could exist without fear."

Cyrus is quiet for a long moment, and my eyes slide open. "Have you ever thought about it?" I ask. My voice is not loud, but it does carry throughout the silent room. "How few of us there are? I can't say that I know any official numbers, but we have estimates. Only 50,000 of us throughout the world. And there are over eight billion humans in it."

I feel sick. I literally have to swallow down bile. If I were human, my hands would tremble. "Think about those odds. You are strong. But if they all knew…if it came to fear for their survival… Do you think we would stand a chance?"

I try to read their faces, to see what they're feeling, thinking. But I'm so terrible at that.

"This isn't about living in fear," I say, shaking my head. "I am not asking you to live in fear. I'm asking you to think of our species. I'm asking you to look for peace."

Through the dead quiet, there's the dinging of someone's phone. A woman with dark skin and a shaved head looks embarrassed as she pulls her phone out to silence it. But she looks at something on her screen, distracted for a moment.

"Old ways of thinking have resurfaced," Cyrus moves on. "And old enemies have come to light once more. Moab believed everything the Blood Father taught him. Lorenzo St. Claire admired the man."

There's another ding that sounds throughout the Great Hall. And then the sound of a vibration.

"Our way of life as we know it will end if we do not put a stop to what is happening outside our borders, now," Cyrus presses on through the distractions.

Another vibration sounds, and this time, Cyrus' eyes ignite red in irritation.

"Your majesties," Malachi speaks up, his eyes slightly wild. "You need to see this." He rises from his seat and crosses to our table. He extends his phone and I take it with sweating palms.

Sound cuts sharply through the Great Hall.

I see a frantic scene, streets crowded with people. Dozens, maybe hundreds. The noise is just a jumbled mess of sound. A man carries the camera, pointing it at himself for a moment, smiling, sticking his tongue out. He flips it back around.

There are two men fighting now. One takes a swing at the other, but he dodges out of the way. Another swing, and it knocks one of the men clean off his feet. He flies back, landing a good fifteen feet away, stopped only by the surrounding crowd.

"Where did you find this?" Cyrus demands as we continue to watch.

"It was posted online an hour ago," Malachi says. "A member of my House just stumbled upon it and sent it to me."

I have no doubt that this is why so many phones were going off in alarm just moments ago. It was getting discovered and shared around the world like wildfire.

The man holding the camera laughs with the crowd, and he darts off through the masses again.

I hear whimpering, and it grows louder as the man walks. "No," a woman cries. "Please, not again."

We see her through the crowd suddenly, and there are two other women grasping her. Suddenly they bury their faces into her neck, fangs flashing and lengthening.

"This is on the Internet?" Cyrus growls, "for anyone to see?"

I watch in horror as the woman's face goes slack as the numbing toxins take her over. The two female vampires suck and pull. The woman grows paler.

The man holding the camera just snickers, thoroughly entertained.

The human woman's knees just give out and she drops as the man pans the view away.

"It looks like it," someone says. "There's…" They swear under their breath. "There's already ten thousand views and it's climbing by the second."

Cyrus grips the back of the chair he stands behind and squeezes. The wood splinters.

The man makes his way through the crowd again, and I don't miss as here and there, we can see other humans being fed upon. He calls out, and another man suddenly looks over, right at the camera. The man says something in a language I don't recognize. The other male laughs, and suddenly, his eyes flash brilliant red.

My heart sinks.

This man, he's showing us everything.

The brute strength.

The blood drinking.

The red eyes.

There, for only a fraction of a second, I see a familiar face walk past in the frame.

"Lorenzo," Cyrus hisses.

But he's gone just as quickly.

The cameraman calls out something loudly, and a few more voices echo back the same words to him. But he carries on.

A circle of vampires stand around a pack of people that I have no doubt are human. Like they're sheep and the vampires are guard dogs. The man says something, and a vampire turns, pulls a young man from the group and hands him over.

The cameraman pulls the young man in, and the video cuts out as he sinks his fangs into his neck.

"It's up to twenty thousand views now," a quiet voice says, but everyone in this big room hears it.

I want to shake my head. The words no, *no* are trapped in my throat.

But I'm just frozen. I'm ice. Rooted on the spot.

"Not everyone will believe what they see," a voice says through the quiet. I recognize it was Hector Valdez.

"But with this many views..." another woman says, one I don't know. "They're going to wonder why this is drawing so much attention. They'll question if it's fake."

I can feel him—Cyrus' presence at my side. I feel him... growing. Filling the room.

For thousands of years, secrecy has been what he valued most. And now, here, it's all being wrecked.

His hand clamps down on the phone, and it crushes, crackling and splitting, dropping to the table in a hundred little pieces.

"Arm yourselves, my children," he seethes. "Come dark, we begin this war."

CHAPTER 9

"There still have been no sightings of Lorenzo or Moab?" Cyrus demands again as he slings his sword around his waist.

"No, your majesty," the spy admits. "We have our suspicions that they are staked out in the inn, but if they've come out, they've been disguised, or simply lost in the crowd."

"They've obviously come out," Cyrus seethes as he helps me cinch the vest around myself. It's filled with weapons. "The man was caught on video."

"My deepest apologies, my grace," the spy says, bowing his head. I can see from the fear in his eyes, he expects to be beheaded or something worse.

But Cyrus cannot afford to lose his temper and punish those who are trying to assist him right now. This is a new game, one I know he doesn't like playing, where he needs to stay in their favor, too.

"It would explain why all of this is so disorganized and

chaotic," I say when Cyrus finishes strapping me in. I slip a stake into one of the pockets, along with a knife. "They have to know that we're looking to take both of them out, so of course they're hiding. But it's hard to manage their people and organize a war when they're in hiding."

Cyrus nods in agreement. "How well armed are they?"

"They've been making stakes," the spy says as Cyrus and I continue to arm ourselves. "They've sent others out to secure weapons, but we've taken every one of their runners out, so far."

"And how many has that been?" I ask as I slip another knife in my boot.

"Eleven, my Queen," he informs. "But those who have arrived, who seem to be allied with Moab, they arrived fully armed."

"We need to take out the airport," I say as I clip two grenades to my belt. "We can't afford to let their numbers grow any larger and they're coming in through that airport. I know they'll find another way, but at least we can slow them down."

The spy nods. "I will take care of it."

The only way we can truly make the airport unusable, is to make it so no one can land on the airstrip.

Explosions are in order.

Noise will be made.

The exposure will widen.

"We will be on the march in thirty minutes," Cyrus says, finished arming himself. "On my mark, I want every sniper we have to fire. I want what little element of surprise we have."

"Yes, your majesty," the spy says, taking a deep bow, and dismissing himself from the armory.

I turn to Cyrus, trying to read the expression on his face. He seems tired, but also…resolved. Prepared.

I remember that look on his face from over a thousand years ago. When we fought very nearly this same war.

"This won't be resolved tonight," I say. "Or tomorrow."

Cyrus reaches for me, wrapping me in his arms. I tuck my head under his chin. "No," he confirms. "It won't. But we will fight it. However long it takes."

"We need to focus on finding Moab and Lorenzo," I say. "If we can cut the legs of this war off, maybe we can end it quicker without so many lives lost."

Cyrus doesn't say anything for a moment, and I feel him physically grow harder.

"Every bit of this must be ended," Cyrus says, still holding me close. "If we do not want history to repeat itself over and over and over again, we must end every bit of this."

The words make my stomach sink, make me feel sick. Because what he's saying is that every one of them going against us must be killed. They all must die.

I can hardly breathe at the thought. So many lives lost. So much contention and hate. Everyone in this war wants some-thing different, and I'm starting to find it difficult to tell who is right and who is wrong.

"It is time," I say. Because it's all I can do. Walk up to this, and face it nose to nose. I step away from the embrace of my fiancé, my husband, depending on who I am at the moment. I turn, and walk down the hall toward the castle gates.

We don't have enough numbers. We really don't.

We have 380 here now with all of the Royals who have arrived from around the world.

We're leaving forty of them here to defend the castle.

We are 340 going up against 498.

Shit.

There are already dozens standing at the gates of the castle when Cyrus and I arrive. They're quiet, reflective. I see determined expressions on their faces. I see death. I see wrath.

I walk out the gates, standing in the street. My eyes go to the mouth of the canyon.

There is no longer any trace of the human army. They're long gone. Our gatekeepers have left, and now nothing stands in the way of Lorenzo and Moab.

They're still waiting. Still gathering.

I hear footsteps gathering behind us. I hear mutters of encouragement. Mutters of disdain. They talk of politics and friends gathered and still missing.

But my eyes remain fixed on that canyon and the road I know is there, leading to a hoard who has already shifted our landscape.

"Tonight marks the beginning of a change," I say. Not loudly. I'm mostly talking to myself. But I know the others hear me when they instantly fall quiet. "Our immortal world has remained unchanged for thousands of years. But tonight, this is the beginning of a new world."

I turn, looking back at them. They're all gathered now. They watch me expectantly. Ready.

"If we come out victorious or if we fall tonight or in a

month, I am by your side," I say. "And I thank you for being by my side."

I see some of them place their fists over their hearts.

We are family here.

Through blood.

Through cause.

"For the future of peace!" Cyrus suddenly bellows, raising his sword into the air.

And as one, every single vampire sets through town, and toward that canyon.

Everything is a blur as we dart, too fast to see clearly. The town is instantly gone. And we're rounding the lake.

Cyrus raises his radio to his lips, calling to our spies. Just as we dart into the mouth of the canyon, Cyrus makes the call.

"Now!"

We're moving at lightning speeds. And just as I make out the crowd in the village, I hear the sky rip apart with the sounds of gunfire.

Bodies stagger back. Men and women drop to the ground. Shot after shot is fired.

And then the Royals collide with the horde, and the guns stop.

And the night is filled with the sound of clanging metal and screams.

I swing a sword as I rush toward a man. I slice up, cutting him open from naval to chin, spilling his guts. I spin just a second later, lopping the head off of a woman with the same colored eyes as my own.

To my side, I see Cyrus, a tornado of blades and brilliantly red eyes. He causes havoc and sends blood spraying in all directions.

The line, the division between the two sides begins to bleed together. Our people push and surge their way through the line. The horde fights back, pushing their way into our ranks.

More of them are armed than I expected. I thought we would be met with stakes against swords. But many of them are armed with swords or shotguns or rifles. Shots ring out into the night.

But there, finally, I hear the sound I was waiting to hear.

An explosion. Dust rises into the air, and sirens sound for just a few moments before being silenced.

We've taken out the airport.

There will be no more Born arriving tonight.

A scream rips from my lungs as I turn, swinging my sword at another young man with yellow-green eyes.

"Do not fight us, sister!" he calls to me as he swings his own sword, fighting only in defense. "Join us in a new world. Do not fade away with the old one!"

"How many innocents will die in this new world?" I bellow, striking at him with blow after blow. "How much blood will be shed?"

He spins, parrying my shot. And I don't quite jump out of the way quick enough. The tip of his sword grazes my left shoulder, splitting the skin, nicking muscle.

With a grunt, I dart forward, kicking my foot in to the center of his chest. He falls backward, hitting the ground, hard. Raising my sword, I bury it in his chest, sinking deep into his heart.

To my side, I see Edmond dart forward, lopping off the head of a woman charging toward me. I nod my head to him in thanks when he looks back at me for a brief moment.

Turning, I search for my next target, and freeze for a moment in fear.

It isn't easy to tell who is the enemy and who is on our side. We all look the same. Are dressed similarly.

The only clear indicator is the eyes of my half-siblings.

I have no way to tell now if the others are Born or Royal.

There, sneaking up on a member of the House of Ng, I see one of my half-siblings. I drop into a slight crouch before launching myself into the air, raising my sword. On my descent, I swing it down.

It connects with the top of her head and keeps sliding down. Through her. Down through her skull. Down through her torso. Down between her legs.

She collapses to the ground, the two separate pieces of her landing with a wet slopping sound.

Find Lorenzo. Find Moab.

Those four words rattle through the back of my brain. These are the priorities. This is our main goal.

I shove my way through the crowd. The spies suspect they're hiding out at the inn. I have to get there.

I slash and slice my way through the crowd, and hear Cyrus fighting to get to my side. But he grows farther away.

I've just cut the sword arm off of one of Lorenzo's children when the sound pricks in my ears. A rush of air. The chopping of blades. I whack down another enemy, turning to search for the source of the sound.

Suddenly, in a blaze of blinding light, a helicopter circles into view. I hold up a hand, blocking out the blinding floodlight.

I look straight up into a camera.

Huge and commercial, it aims at me clearly. Only a moment later, it pans out over the crowd.

It could be broadcasting live.

I turn to look and see what viewers might be witnessing, right now.

Hundreds of bodies. Numbering over eight hundred. They swing at one another with swords—primitive and gleaming. There are gunshots being fired. There are individuals fighting, ripping one another limb from limb with bare hands.

There are fangs everywhere.

Most eyes are lit brilliant red.

It's a brawl, fought with inhuman strength.

And that camera is recording it all.

The battle has stilled for a moment, everyone in shock at the sight of the helicopter, hovering just twenty feet over the ground. They're temporarily blinded by the floodlight.

And then one vampire launches at the helicopter. Tossed into the air by others, a member of Court, catches hold of the feet of the chopper. And then there's another. Not wasting a second, they climb into the cockpit.

It tilts dangerously to the right, and launches to the side, toward the airport.

I smile. One tiny victory. We need that.

Even if the damage has already been done and it's too late to recover.

Five seconds later, the helicopter crashes.

I turn to return to the battle, when an iron cuff clamps down over my right wrist, knocking my sword from my hand. In the same moment, something dark and flexible is pulled over my head, and cinched tight around my neck.

In my moment of surprise, taken off guard, my other wrist is wrenched behind my back, and another cuff snaps around my left wrist.

My assailants don't hesitate a second. They knock me off my feet, and drag me off.

I scream.

I yell.

I make death threats.

I sling every curse word I know.

But there are four of them dragging me away, containing me.

"Cyrus will have every one of your entrails spread across the world for this!" I threaten.

I feel the air grow cold.

And we're going down stairs. Boots sound over hard concrete.

The air smells damp and old.

A cellar. We have to be in a cellar.

I'm shoved backward, and my internal organs panic, preparing to brace myself to fall to the ground, but my spine jolts when I fall into a chair, nearly tipping out of it, my vampire instincts the only things keeping me from ending up on the floor.

The second I'm down, my hands are yanked to the sides. My arms are pulled straight and tight, balancing me centered.

From behind, I feel something touch my back, right over my heart. And another touches my chest.

I take a breath of air as the bag is yanked from off my head. My hair falls across my face, temporarily blocking my view.

A figure takes a step toward me. He's not alone. The four who dragged me here surround me, too. Two of them hold stakes at my front and back. The other two must be the ones who chained my wrists and secured them to the hooks in the floor.

The figure in front of me stoops and carefully moves my hair from my face, attempting to right it.

I know exactly who it is before he clears my view.

I can smell him.

I can feel him.

And then there are his golden-jade eyes, looking into the ones he gave me.

"Hello, Sevan," he says with a little smile.

He's controlling his smugness. I can tell in every muscle under the skin of his face. And I hate him for it. I want to shred every one of them to pieces and make tacos out of them.

"You will regret this, Lorenzo," I seethe. "Every bit of your existence the past seven hundred years, but especially this."

"You don't even hear three words from me before you begin the threats?" he says, dragging a chair across the floor. He sets it in front of me and sits in it backwards, draping his forearms across the back of it. "Though I will say, I've never heard anyone who makes more creative threats than Cyrus, until you came here, Logan Pierce."

"I haven't even tried," I say spitefully.

He smiles at that, a little smirk.

Yep. Tacos. With cheese and lettuce and really spicy sauce.

"I would quake in fear, but you're the one in the chair and chains, and I'm the one with all the numbers on ground level."

"From what I hear, things aren't going so peacefully and smoothly," I say. I lean forward. "How is my first grandson doing these days?"

I get him there. The expression on his face sobers. His jaw tightens. He sits back in his chair.

"Did you know that he was still alive?" he asks. And from his tone, I know he genuinely wonders at the answer.

I take a breath, considering how I should answer. Since I cannot see any grave harm in telling him, I decide to go with the truth.

"I had forgotten," I say. "But I remembered a guard telling us he had escaped, a long time ago. But no, I didn't consciously know he was still out in the world until a few days ago."

"He's going to be a problem," Lorenzo says, his eyes sliding over to meet mine again. "He's going to throw kinks in all my plans."

"You poor thing," I say, throwing false pity into my tone.

"You should care about this," Lorenzo says, sitting forward. "Our visions for the future... His looks much more red than mine does."

My blood does go cold at that. Lorenzo wants to unite all vampires, to make the "family" stronger. If that means exposing all our kind, so be it.

But Moab. Moab worshiped my son, would do whatever he wished.

And my son's greatest wish was to show the world what we are. He didn't want to hide. He wanted to break out of secrecy and show the world just how strong he was.

Moab will ruin the world.

"He needs to die," I state, my tongue slipping before my brain can pre-screen my words.

"Yes, he does," Lorenzo says. "As soon as possible. Before he screws anything else up."

"Are you asking for my help?" I ask, my brows furrowing at the realization.

His eyes flick up to mine again, and he doesn't say anything for a long moment. "The enemy of my enemy is my friend, isn't that what they say?"

"You can never be my friend when you're attempting mutiny against me," I say, not trying to contain my sneer.

"Not even for a few days, perhaps a week or two?" Lorenzo says as he leans forward, bracing his forearms on his knees. "Not even if it means taking out an enemy who wants to turn the whole world into a living hell?"

I want to smash something. Something really nice. Something really pretty and expensive. Just to fully punctuate how much I want to scream, how much I hate this corner I'm painted into.

"You understand that I'm still going to try and kill you, the first chance I get, if we succeed in taking Moab out or not, right?" I say, leaning forward just a bit, the tip of the stake one of my half-siblings holds pressing into my chest.

"Oh, of course," Lorenzo says. "And as soon as we've killed Moab, I'm going right back to finding every way I can to lock your husband in the deepest pit on the planet Earth. And you may be my daughter, but you're one of many, so if you continue to stand in my way, I'll do what is necessary."

"Good," I say, sitting straight and tall. "As long as we understand one another. I have some ideas."

CHAPTER 10

SHOULDER TO SHOULDER IN THE DARK STAIRWAY, I LOOK over at my enemy—my father. His jade-yellow eyes meet my jade-yellow eyes.

There's animosity in every centimeter of each of our eyes. We'd stake each other right here and now. We'd rip one another's hearts from each other's chests.

But for this moment, for just a few days, we need one another.

One problem at a time.

So together, we push the door open.

We step out, side by side.

Lorenzo lifts a horn to his lips, just like he stepped out of the fifth century, and bellows it.

The second the sound dies away, I cup my hands around my mouth, and scream as loudly as I can, "Allies of the Crown, retreat!"

Two calls, both signaling our armies to turn and run from the fight.

Lorenzo bellows his horn once more, and I scream my command again.

I turn, my eyes searching. There, across the battlefield, I see Cyrus.

His eyes jump from me, to Lorenzo, who is now running with a crowd, all his children retreating, running further into the canyon, away from the battle, and further from the castle.

There's a thousand questions in Cyrus' eyes. But there's even more trust. So he yells "retreat" with me, and watches as our people disengage from the battle, and run back toward home.

I back toward Cyrus, my eyes scanning the battlefield.

Moab. Moab. Where are you, Moab?

There are just as many staying, stranded in the middle, as there are running away from the fight. They stay with weapons, some still firing, looking confused and disoriented as the battle suddenly dissolves.

A little smile pulls on my face as I turn, jogging toward Cyrus. I stoop momentarily, retrieving my sword that was forced from my hand earlier.

Cyrus gives me a confused, questioning look as I join his side, but he doesn't demand answers, just follows me, as I run with our people toward the mouth of the canyon.

It's killing me, walking away. I want to stay, an invisible little butterfly, innocently fluttering through the tiny, destroyed town. I want to see what's happening.

But I know our spies will have a report for me shortly.

So with my people, my family, we retreat into Roter Himmel.

"We were winning!" someone declares arrogantly as I walk among them, headed toward the gates of the castle. "Why the hell did we run away?"

"Why are Lorenzo's children running like they've given up?" someone else demands.

I ignore them all, walking side by side with Cyrus and finally stopping at the gates of the castle.

"Dorian," I call out. "Malachi."

Through the crowd they both make their way, stopping at my side.

Keeping my voice low, I quickly explain what just happened. My agreement with Lorenzo.

"But we *will* kill him if the opportunity presents itself," Malachi says, not really even a question in his voice.

I shake my head. "If we do that, his children will turn against us again, and they're back to two against one, when it comes to sides and armies. I don't think we can actually afford to go after Lorenzo until we've killed Moab."

"Forced to work with snakes," Cyrus seethes. "Times of war…"

I look at him sympathetically. "I don't like it either. But think about it. Who is the more deadly, experienced enemy here?"

"Moab," Dorian says for him, his face grim and white.

I nod in agreement. "Moab has fought this exact war before. He's led armies, he's won battles before. Lorenzo has no experience in war. I think we can afford to put our problems with him aside in exchange for the benefit of more bodies against the more experienced issue."

"I'm not arguing against you, Sevan," Cyrus says with a sigh. "I just don't have to like it."

I give him a little smile and squeeze his hand. "Okay," I say with a breath. I take a heartbeat to gather my thoughts, and turn back to the crowd waiting for an explanation.

"If we try to fight against everything coming against us all at once we're going to lose."

That sets every single one of them immediately silent. Their expressions slacken. Their eyes widen a bit. They fall utterly still.

"It's true," I say, shaking my head and taking a step forward. "We're vastly outnumbered. I have no idea how well-trained Lorenzo's children are in battle. I hope it isn't much. I can't imagine they've ever fought any wars. But they had to know they were going to fight some day. But I do know Moab's people will be skilled. Moab was raised in war. Thrives off it. So if we have to fight all of them all at once, we're going to lose."

I clasp my fingers around one wrist behind my back, facing the members of Court.

"I've spoken with Lorenzo just minutes ago," I say, and before they can freak out and protest, I move on, even as a few mouths open to speak. "I didn't get much of a choice in it, and trust me, if the opportunity had first presented itself, he would have been dead before he could open his mouth." I glare out at the crowd who is annoyingly questioning me.

"Moab is a problem for Lorenzo. They both want essentially the same thing, and he can't stand that. So he asked me to set our own problems aside for a moment."

"You're teaming up with that betraying bastard?" someone accuses from the crowd.

"Do you want to die?" I yell, feeling my eyes ignite red. I take another step forward, every muscle in my body flexed to snap bones. "Because we will. We are strong. But we are so vastly outnumbered. So yes, for a few days, until we can smoke Moab out and kill him, I am teaming up with Lorenzo St. Claire."

"So what is the plan, my Queen?" Cyrus' voice suddenly cuts through the air before anyone else can argue with me.

My nostrils flare, and I have to take a good five seconds to cool myself down. I force my fisted fingers to calm, to relax.

"Lorenzo's people have retreated further into the canyon. With us here at the mouth, we have Moab's remaining army surrounded." I slowly pace back and forth across the road. "I want to hear from our spies what is happening right now. Moab has been in hiding, and I pray with this sudden withdrawal, with the confusion, that he will have to show his face to investigate what is going on."

My eyes turn back toward the mouth of the canyon. I want to be out there. I want to be one of those spies. I want to be the sniper who finally spots him and takes him out.

"If he doesn't show his face within an hour, we will go back, and the battle will resume. Our people, and Lorenzo's, will kill as many of Moab's army as we can. We will take prisoners. We will interrogate. Until one of them reveals Moab's location."

I look over at Cyrus. And I think it's a confirmation I'm looking for there, that I'm doing the right thing. He's done this for so long, on his own and by my side.

I've never been one to make the calls.

But this is my war. For my people. Against my father. This is what I fought for.

Cyrus' expression is difficult to read. I can't tell what's going through his head. But he nods, his eyes hard.

He's with me.

With a plan set in place, the members of Court and the Royals arrived, set to arming themselves once more, taking a rest, a moment to regroup.

Cyrus and I greet the newest arrivals, the House of Koto, from Borneo, arrived just thirty minutes ago. They join the ranks, fully armed, ready to fight.

Static sounds over my radio and I raise it to my ear, listening for the scratchy words.

"No signs of Moab yet," a voice says. I don't know who it is, we have multiple spies watching at all times.

"What's happening up there?" I question instead of letting the frustration and disappointment flood through me.

"They're regrouping," the spy reports. "Counting their dead. They seem pretty panicked that the airport has been destroyed."

My eyes turn to the skies, and I see a plane headed off in the distance. No way to tell though if it was trying to come here. "So they are still expecting more arrivals," I conclude, meeting Cyrus' eyes.

"Safe to say yes," he responds.

I let out a sigh.

How far does this extend? How many of them are there, throughout the world, trying to get to Roter Himmel, so that they can change the world forever?

I have to believe that if we kill Moab, it will cut the head off of this thing. At least for another century.

"Keep us posted if anything changes," I say into the radio. He makes an acknowledgement and the line goes silent once more.

"I'm done waiting," Cyrus says. "I want this to end, tonight." He shifts, checking his sword hanging at his side. He accepts a handful of stakes handed to him by a woman, tucking them into the same belt. "Moab dies, this ends, tonight."

I nod. Turning to the crowd, I take them in, counting once more.

We lost two of us in that first skirmish. How many more would die tonight?

My chest aches at the thought of *anyone* having to die. This all could have stayed so peaceful. Why did anyone have to change any of it?

But this is the price of freedom and peace. It's been repeated in history, over and over again. People die for what they believe in.

The same will be true for all three sides of this war tonight.

I look at the time, ticking down, down, down.

At five minutes to the hour, I step out once more.

"We have no idea where Moab is. In reality, there could be more allied with him, here, than we realize," I pull my sword from it's sheath, turning to face the castle for a moment. "If we lose the castle, we'll lose the war. I want the Royals to stay here. You defend the castle. And if anything happens to the rest of us..." I look out, at the members of Court, "the world will need you."

There are thirty-eight Royals at the castle. Not many. But with the defenses the castle offers, I have to hope that it will be enough to keep the castle from falling.

I look around at the Royals. So many of them I do not know. But there are the few familiar faces. Edmond and Hector Valdez nod at me, standing a little straighter. They will defend the castle.

"Everything will change by morning," Cyrus speaks up, his powerful voice filling the valley. "Lives will be lost tonight." He steps forward, his hand held on the hilt of his sword. "The tides will shift, one way or another. But I swear to you, this is a world worth fighting for. Peace, the cloak of secrecy, is worth fighting for. We are vampires, and we will fight for our survival. Our existence."

Someone cries out, a war cry, loud and determined. Another rips into the air, followed by a chorus of war screams.

And as one, we turn, and once more head back to the battle.

Through the streets of Roter Himmel we rip like the wind of a tornado. Across the valley we dart. Up the street to the mouth of the canyon our feet pound. We flood the road that winds through the mountains.

I hear them. The two or three hundred bodies ahead. Breathing hard, waiting. I hear the clang of metal against metal. I hear the loading of a shotgun.

But as we close in on the town, I suddenly drop to a dead stop, throwing my arms out, stopping Cyrus on my one side and Mina on the other.

There is Moab's army.

But standing there before them, is a line of humans.

I can smell them. All two-dozen of them.

They face us, and every one of them holds a phone up, the flash shining brilliant light in our direction.

"It is time for a new age," a woman says from the crowd. She steps forward, winding her way between people. And as she comes closer, my blood chills.

I know her.

I remember that blonde hair. Her strong frame, her tall stature. I know those capable hands. And I know that scar on her face, running from the top corner of her ear, down to the corner of her nose, cutting across her lips, and disappearing at her chin.

I gave it to her.

Well over a thousand years ago.

"Kala." Her name slips over mine and Cyrus' lips at the same time.

Our second grandchild. Born just after Moab. Just like him in every way.

We thought she had died in the great war.

"The world needs to know what we have been forced to hide for over two thousand years now," she says, standing between two of the humans who hold their phones up. "They need to see what we are. What we can do. What we are capable of. They need to know that there is so much more to this world than them."

My throat constricts. Because I understand.

Every one of those humans is broadcasting live.

Kala steps forward, in view of all of those phones. They each shift to focus on her. "The country of Austria has been holding a secret for thousands of years," she begins. "It may not have started here, but it spread from here. This man," she turns, looking back at Cyrus, "created something incredible. But then he hid it from the world. But that is going to change. Because all of these people, everyone you see is-"

But the air suddenly rushes from her lungs, cutting her words off abruptly.

A huge blade is embedded into her back, and blood instantly runs down her shirt and she collapses to her knees.

Cyrus breathes hard between his teeth, still poised in position from throwing the massive blade.

Some enemies just won't die. Others, you expect to put up a huge fight.

Kala has survived under the radar for nearly two thousand years.

And Cyrus just killed her with no effort.

"Leave," he seethes, though his voice is not loud. "If you value your lives, and the way the world looks, leave."

But the humans don't even get a moment to respond. Because from further down the road, behind this army my grandson has amassed, there are cries and shouts. And the sound of clanging metal.

Bodies shove past the broadcasting humans, swords raised. Others take aim and fire.

It takes only one and a half seconds before the first human drops to the ground, dropping her phone, dead.

I can't save them. There's no protecting them. And there's no hiding what their cameras are about to see.

With blood red eyes, with fangs bared, with brutal, inhuman strength, we have no choice but to surge forward and fight the war that will determine the future of the world.

I swing my sword, digging the blade deep into the side of a man who rushes at me with wild eyes. I spin, yanking it from his ribs, using my momentum and lop his head off just as he raises his own sword.

A shot fires and a woman rushing at me with a stake drops to the ground, her chest a bloody mess.

From the corner of my eye, I spot Cyrus. He's a whirl-wind of arms and blades as he battles two other vampires. With a huff, I dart through the crowd, slicing as I run. With a great scream, I leap through the air, swinging my blade down.

I drive it through the top of one of the men's heads, sinking it down, down, through his throat, into his chest, and I aim for his heart.

I know I've hit it when he collapses to the ground. A spray of blood splashes over my face as Cyrus decapitates the man he fights.

Our enemies slain, we look at one another for a brief moment. A quick check that the other is alright, that we're uninjured.

Other than the burn in my throat that reminds me it's been days since I fed, I feel fine. Great.

I feel a little smile pull on my lips. One tugs on Cyrus' face and he grabs the front of my armor, pulling me to him, and he crushes his lips to mine. It's a possession, a declaration that no matter what, I'm his and he is mine. We're in this together, to whatever the end might be.

Cyrus suddenly yanks me to the side, nearly throwing me off balance, when he raises his sword, and swings wildly at a woman who snuck up at my back. He drives the blade into her stomach, and rips up, cutting her open, and spilling her entrails. He gives a great cry, breathing hard as he looks back at me.

"Don't kiss me again out here," I say with a smirk. "You'll get me killed with those lips."

Cyrus doesn't smile, and know to him it isn't the least bit funny, but I turn, a smile on my swollen lips, and search for my next victim.

I'm covered in blood from head to foot as I battle Born after Born. I've lost track of the bodies I've fell. Somewhere between fifteen and fifty. It becomes difficult to navigate through the battlefield, there are so many bodies littering the ground.

Bodies of Moab's people, bodies of Court members. Bodies of my half-siblings.

Bodies of those stupid humans who had no idea what they were getting mixed up in, or how little Moab and Kala's army cared what would become of them.

Realizing how many bodies were falling, and exactly zero answers I had, I grab the next Born I come across, yanking her toward me, nose to nose as I knock the stake from her hands.

"Where is Moab hiding?" I ask calmly, even though we're nose to nose, my sword pressed into her navel.

"Right under your nose," she says with a smile. "Can't you find him?"

I yank her a little tighter to me, and the tip of my sword sinks into her stomach an inch or two. "I'm not a fan of vague answers," I say quietly into her ear. I back up, looking into her eyes. "I want specifics. An exact location."

She laughs, shaking her head, oblivious to any pain my penetrating blade is causing. "It doesn't matter where Moab is. It doesn't matter how long you fight against us. The world knows now. They've seen. And everything has already changed."

My stomach has disappeared. My body feels cold.

I know how the world works now. I know what technology is capable of accomplishing. I know the power of the internet and social media and the news.

There were two-dozen humans live-streaming on our side. I have to assume there were another two dozen of them on Lorenzo's side.

Forty-eight humans spreading the word is all it would take to set the world on fire in this modern age.

With a loud scream and a grunt, I shove my hand forward and up, burying my blade into her chest, piercing her heart.

I don't even give her a second look as she collapses to the ground, dead.

Looking around the battlefield, I see Cyrus holding a man to the ground, a blade pressed into the soft spot under his chin, interrogating him. Only a few moments later, he buries the blade into the man's brain.

Others from Court are using words, attempting to gain information about Moab's whereabouts.

Where are you hiding, Moab?

And suddenly, there, tickling the back of my brain, there's something.

Something I nearly forgot, even though it was traumatizing in the moment.

A snow-white scalp.

Sitting in Cyrus crown on his desk chair.

Moab's signature move.

Moab had been in the castle.

What if...

What if...?

I turn, my eyes going to the mouth of the canyon, even though it's miles away. My brain traces the path back along the road, down the valley, past the lake, into stone walls.

What if...

Moab escaped hundreds of years ago.

No one knew how.

All entrances to the castle were watched round the clock under normal circumstances.

Where is he?

Right under your nose.

But there was one entrance, one I thought only Cyrus and I knew about. It wasn't us who had created it.

What if there were more ways to access it than just the one I knew about?

What if...?

My eyes turn back to the battlefield. Golden-jade eyes flash from everywhere, and side-by-side, the members of Court fight with them to destroy Moab's army.

But in my gut, there is a feeling.

We haven't been able to find Moab, because he isn't here.

"No," I mutter under my breath. "No."

All my organs turn to ash. My feet start moving before I can logically plan anything. Before I can take a second to think. Before I can give four words—*back to the castle*—as an order to my people.

I just start running.

CHAPTER 11

I SEE PERFECTLY CLEAR AS I RUN, AN INVISIBLE BLUR. MY feet are numb within seconds from pounding the ground so hard. My hair rips from its braid, flowing out behind me.

I crest the road, the valley coming into view.

I hear a scream. I hear glass shatter.

It comes from the castle.

A curse and a prayer slips over my lips as I race down the road.

"No," I cry, so, so desperate and sick. "No."

I bullet toward the lake, to the southeast corner. I don't slow as I leap into the air, forming an arrow with my body, and dive into the water.

The cold hits me like a baseball bat, but I use every ounce of strength I have to propel myself through the water. I rocket through the dark, frigid water, knowing exactly where I'm going.

Even with my enhanced vision, I can hardly see the dark hole. I rely on memory more than sight.

There, deep, along the cliff of the shore, I find the entrance to the cave.

The rock cuts back into the shore, creating an underwater tunnel. I swim through it for a good fifteen yards, dragging my hands along the roof of it, and finally, there, I find the opening.

A narrow circle opens above my head, and I pull myself up and out of the water, onto a muddy ledge. Gasping for oxygen that I don't really need, I pull myself up into the cold air.

A tunnel, barely tall enough for me not to have to crouch to walk, cuts from here at the lake's edge, and drives back straight toward the castle.

It's pitch black. I can't see anything. So I walk slowly. I have to inspect the entire thing. I have to know if there are any other entrances to the castle beside the one I know.

It feels like it goes on and on forever, and I have to remind myself, the tunnel is in fact nearly two miles long. But I don't cheat, I don't skip anything. I have to find any other entrances. I have to know.

The entry that I know of into the castle is directly ahead. It cuts down into the castle and comes out in the secret armory in the floor of my bedroom. Even though this tunnel feels infinitely long, I know that there are exactly sixty-seven more steps before the tunnel makes a slight left bend and then begins rising.

I drag my hand along the tunnel, breathing hard, using

my enhanced senses to listen to the sound reverberate against the walls.

My hand drops into cold air at the same time I hear a sound that doesn't belong.

Three footsteps.

I halt my breathing and follow my hand into the unknown entry. I have to crouch down as my forehead hits the dirt ceiling. I tuck myself against the wall and place my hand on the hilt of my sword.

Straining, I listen hard for more footsteps, for breathing.

There's one, but then no more. And then another.

They're coming toward me, from the direction of the lake.

Someone followed me.

They're deathly quiet. I only hear a footstep every thirty or so feet they travel.

I count in my head, imagining myself stepping through the dark to gauge when they should level with this side tunnel I just stepped into.

And just as they step level with me, I draw my sword and swing.

A huge hand wraps around my wrist, stopping my swing instantly. A finger presses to my lips before I can say anything and a low voice whispers in the dark.

"It is me, my Queen," they say, not letting go of me so I cannot use that sword, or the stake in my other hand to kill him.

"Larkin," I breathe. My heart is going a million miles an hour, making it hard to breathe.

He makes a quiet affirmative noise. "The issue you asked me to take care of has been dealt with." It feels like forever ago, when there were Born who had gotten into Roter Himmel and planned the attack on Cyrus that led to him being decapitated. There had been four of them. One of them had betrayed the others, killing them, and then fled. I told Larkin to track them down and not return until the problem was eliminated.

I knew he would succeed.

"You just got back?" I whisper.

"Just moments ago," he says. "I came through the mountains, and was on my way to the castle when I saw you run straight from the canyon to the lake. You looked as if you needed assistance."

"I do," I say with an appreciative nod I know he can't see. "We're fighting Moab's army right now, with Lorenzo's aide for the time being. But we haven't seen any signs of the man himself yet. I think..." I really didn't want to think what I thought. "I think he's inside the castle."

A booming sound echoes through the tunnel and I can't stand here and explain any longer. I take off through my newly discovered branch, dragging my hands along the walls to guide me.

By my estimates we have a quarter of a mile left to go before we will be under the castle. I count down the steps in my head.

And when I get down to fifteen, I feel the air shift.

"There's an opening up ahead," Larkin whispers very, very quietly.

I nod my head in agreement. I draw my sword again.

Slowly, we creep through the tunnel and my heart hammers faster as the rush of air grows steadier.

Faint, faint light cuts through the ceiling of the tunnel up ahead, and I slow as I come to stand beneath it.

It's a pile of rubble. I reach out with my sword, prodding at it, and immediately, a pile of rocks falls from up above and scatters across the tunnel floor. I reach up, digging through the rubble. It goes at an upward angle. And after about a foot of digging, my arm suddenly breaks free into open space.

I look back at Larkin, only barely able to see part of his face through the dark.

He cups his hands and I place my foot into it, and he gives me a lift.

I find myself in a dug out hole, three feet deep, six feet in length. Above that opens into a big space, lit with torches along the walls, with a wide tunnel with stairs rising up.

Just to the side of this coffin built into the stone floor, is a massive boulder, multiple tons in size.

My jaw slackens.

Moab's prison.

When Cyrus captured him after the war, he had Moab brought here, to this specifically designed prison. A hole in the ground, where Moab had lain for sixteen centuries before somehow miraculously escaping.

"This was Moab's prison," I say as Larkin climbs through the little hole at the end where Moab's head would have lain. "He...he was here for hundreds of years. He..." I look back to the tiny hole we escaped through.

"He dug himself straight through the rock," I said. "That tunnel, it was just a foot under the bedrock. He..." I shake my head. "Moab simply walked out of the castle to escape and found his freedom through the lake."

The sound of metal against stone draws both of our eyes to the stairway.

"I think we know exactly how he got back into the castle," Larkin says aloud.

There's a shrill scream, and when it triples in volume and fear, I realize it's not just one person screaming, but multiple. Four, five.

"Come on!" I say, forgetting instantly to keep my voice down.

As always, Larkin is armed to the teeth, even if it isn't immediately visible. He pulls out two fighting blades, and we race up the stairs together.

The stairs rise before flattening out, and we dart through a long tunnel. Moab's prison was carved into the darkest heart of the mountain. Away from the world he so longed to take over. So through an incredibly long tunnel we travel, before we reach another set of stairs.

They're steep and are nearly more like a ladder.

"There is a hatch just up above," I whisper to Larkin, who climbs behind me. "It opens into a supply closet. We just have to hope and pray it's unoccupied."

He makes a small noise, acknowledging what I just said.

I rise four more stairs, holding my hand above my head. In the pitch black, I can't see a thing.

And there's the hatch. I rise up one more stair, pressing my ear to the smooth wood, listening.

There are still sounds of the ambush, but I don't hear anyone in the space above us, so I slowly lift the hatch.

The room is empty. Where it should be filled to the brim with supplies, all the boxes have been pushed away from the hatch, things toppled over. Like a lot of people came in through that little entry into the castle.

"Shit," I breathe.

Larkin surfaces behind me and we both silently creep to the door.

Peering through the crack, I see a woman from the House of Cordero locking swords with a man. He pushes her back down the hall.

She slips, getting knocked down to one knee.

I don't think.

I'm so stupid.

I dart from the room, silent and unexpected. I bring my sword down, cutting clean through his skull, slicing it right down the middle. He drops to the ground in a bloody heap.

My head whips around, surveying the scene, looking for others, as the woman breathes my name and a profuse *thank you*.

We're in a hallway on the fourth floor, a little way down from the main stairway that goes up to the main floor.

I turn, grabbing the Cordero woman by the front of her shirt and drag her back toward Larkin and the room we just came through.

"Sevan," the woman breathes. "Thank...thank you."

"How many of Moab's people are in the castle?" I demand, ignoring her.

"We..." she struggles to focus, to think back through the events of the last hour or two. "We were spread throughout the castle, guarding the entry points. I was on the third floor when suddenly all these people poured up the stairs."

"How many?" I demand again. "Twenty people? A hundred?"

"I'd guess fifty or so," she says. Her eyes are wide and keep flicking back to the door. She's totally overwhelmed.

"And how many of us are dead?" I ask the question I do not want to ask. "Do you have any guess?"

Tears prick her eyes. She shakes her head. "I don't know. They took us off guard, coming at us from inside the castle."

I sigh through my nose, frustrated that she can't keep it together in this moment.

"Larkin and I are going into the castle," I say. "I need you to stay here." I grab her sword, which she dropped in the doorway and hand it back to her. "This," I say as I point down at the hatch, "is how they all got inside. I want you watching this hatch, and if anyone tries to come through it, you hack them to pieces. Got it?"

She takes two quick breaths through her pursed lips, collecting herself, and finally nods.

I don't have time to make sure she can actually handle this. I just have to hope she can be the leader she's always been.

"Any grand ideas on how to clear them out of the castle?" I breathe to Larkin as we go back to the door.

"With them spread throughout the castle, there's no quick way to do it," he says, his eyes scanning the narrow sliver of hall we can see. "Our best bet is to go room by room, as quickly as we can, and stick together. Then we pray we find individuals and can take them out between the two of us."

I swear under my breath. "It feels like a shit plan."

"It is," Larkin agrees. "But it's the only option at the moment."

Without waiting for my confirmation, Larkin slips out the door, waving me after him.

We slip down the hall, hooking to the central space of the fourth floor: the kitchens.

The main cooking area is clear, as is the walk-in refrigerator and freezer. As we round a corner, Larkin holds up a fist, halting me for a moment.

I hear it, too. The sound of someone inside the pantry.

Larkin darts inside. Whoever it was doesn't even get half a second to make a cry. I can only see Larkin's back. Then I hear the wet sound of a blade sinking into a body, and then that body hitting the ground.

With the kitchens cleared, we move deeper into the fourth floor.

Two great ballrooms are set on the north and south sides of the stairs. The first is clear. But in the south, we find an all-out brawl.

In the chaos, I see Edmond Valdez, locked in a sword fight with a man who has half his face sliced off. Edmond is back-to-back with two other Royals I don't recognize. Five of Moab's men appear to be winning.

There's three dead people on the ground.

Neither Larkin nor I hesitate. We're both across the ballroom in a fraction of a second. I lop the head off the man Edmond was fighting, and Larkin slices two women through in one clean sweep.

With the tides turned, the other two are swiftly killed.

"Apparently today is going to be a day of timing," Edmond says, breathing hard. He pushes his hair out of his face, leaving behind a streak of blood. "Thank you."

My eyes go to the two others at Edmond's side. I recognize one from the House of Ng, but I can't place the other. But almost immediately, my eyes go to the two dead on the floor.

"Ines and Adele," I breathe, kneeling down beside them.

From the House of Emile, in France.

"They were the last of the Emile family," Hector breathes. He shakes his head. "The line ended when their father produced two daughters. What...what will become of their House now?"

My throat is thick. So, so tight. Emotions stab the backs of my eyes as I look at the two women.

Their faces are so peaceful looking now, like they're sleeping. Except there's so much blood.

"We will have to worry about that later," I say. The words sound all wrong coming from a throat this constricted. "We have to go help others."

"Stay together," Larkin instructs.

I have to leave. I have to look away from the Emile girls. Because my brain wants to spin out.

One whole House now is destroyed. The ramifications will be huge for their area.

A whole House.

But I can't think about that right now.

There are dozens of personal quarters on this level. As a team, one by one, we go through the rooms, checking for anyone.

We find the body of Siobhan O'Rourke in one of the bedrooms. Another House leader, dead.

There are also the bodies of five Born scattered throughout the rooms, their heads removed, or stakes or blade holes through their hearts.

Sure the fourth floor is clear, as a group of five, we ascend the stairs to the main level.

The carnage is so much worse here.

I spot no less than seven Royals lying dead on the floor just from the stairs. There are another twelve Born dead.

But a battle rages at the front gates.

We don't wait. We react. We jump into the battle.

I swing this sword like I've never fought in any other lifetime.

I have a cut down the middle of my back. Blood is pouring down my chin from a slice on my cheek. I nearly lost the fingers on my left hand, and now have a huge gash down the back of my knuckles.

But I keep swinging.

I take two of Moab's soldiers down.

And scream in regret as a man from the House of Ng goes down, instantly turning ashen gray.

With a war scream, I thrust my sword, burying it in a woman's chest.

"Where is Moab?" I bellow, to anyone who may hear me.

Find Moab. End this. The words chant through my head.

But I don't get a reply.

Our battle spreads throughout the entry of the castle. I go back-to-back with Larkin, swinging and slicing and bleeding all over the place.

I see Edmond out of the corner of my eye as he cuts the head from a soldier, only to catch his heel on something and trip backward.

There's a choked off scream that doesn't fully escape his lips. "Raphael?"

I dare a look in his direction for just half a second.

Edmond is crouched on the ground next to a body. Through the blood, I recognize the face of Raphael Valdez.

"Raphael?" Edmond cries in horror.

I lose the rest of the words he cries as I strike at the soldier before me. Again and again I blow. I slice through the air, dart out of the way of his blade. And when he doesn't take a big enough step to the side, I bury my sword into his side, sinking the tip all the way to his heart.

I hear a skull crunch against stone behind me and know Larkin has slain the betrayer.

I take one breath, two, nearly deafened by the pounding sound of my own heart. And the quiet.

Looking around, I see that we've cleared the entry.

Every soldier now lies dead.

Still standing are six Royals, me, Larkin, and a grieving Edmond.

A voice, muffled and barely audible trickles to my ears. And my body instantly feels hollow.

"He ordered the extermination sixteen years ago."

Very quietly, I hear her voice.

No.

I take a step toward the hall. My footsteps echo on the stone floor. Bloody boot prints follow after me.

"And did all these Houses instantly obey?"

Another voice floats to my ears, one I don't recognize.

"It..." she falters. "It wasn't an active execution of the order. It more came about as they caused issues. At least in my area. We took them out when they stepped out of line. A few of my House members were more...assertive whenever they came across them. But it took years. A decade, really, before finding any of them became a real challenge."

The massive doors stand before me, and beyond them, there is the soaring space of the Great Hall.

"Sevan?" Larkin says, a question and a request to come back in his voice.

I take the final four steps, and enter the Hall.

The great table is still set in the middle of the space. Fifty chairs surround it. But only three people are seated at it, on the end furthest from me.

The moment I clear the doors, they slam shut behind me, sealing me inside. I don't have to turn and look to know that there were two soldiers waiting inside, prepared to close them as soon as I walked in.

Instantly, I hear Larkin and others at the door, pounding on it, yelling my name.

At the noise, three pairs of eyes jump to my face.

There's a woman there, she looks familiar, but I can't quite place her. She's pretty, I'd guess in her mid-forties. Her blonde hair is cut short and blunt, accentuating her sharp but balanced features.

Sitting across the table from her, in front of the camera set up on the table, is Alivia Conrath. She looks at me with horror, her eyes begging me to run.

Because seated at the head of the table, just beside her, is Moab.

My heat stops.

It literally stops beating in my chest for a couple of seconds.

Because it is Moab, but just as his name means, *of his father*, he looks just like his father. Just like the Blood Father. Just like my son.

Dark green eyes. Like Cyrus'. A slightly too-full upper lip. Like Cyrus'.

Curly hair falls onto his forehead. Like his father's hair. Just like Sevan's hair. A square jaw, just like his father's, just like his grandmother's.

I may not have the same face anymore. I may look entirely different from when I was born as Sevan in the country that is now known as Armenia.

But our son was the perfect blend of Cyrus and I. And Moab looks just like him.

"Hello, All Mother," he says.

CHAPTER 12

My brain is screaming over and over and over.

Too much.

Too much to process in here.

The camera.

Alivia.

Moab.

This mystery woman.

And, oh shit…the pile of decapitated bodies on the floor just five feet to Moab's right side.

If I were human, I'd turn and throw up, all over the floor. Because there's a pile of…hair. Scalps. Just to the side of the pile of bodies. And every one of those bodies, those dead Royals, is missing theirs.

"Why don't you come join us, grandmother?" Moab invites.

The sly smile on his face and the soldiers behind me who

step up and tighten around me tell me this is not an invitation. It's a command.

I cross the room, holding my head high, my lips pressed in a thin line. I tighten my grip on my sword, which still drips blood to the floor. My eyes meet Alivia's momentarily, and she does nothing to hide her terror. Her eyes are wide and wild. There's sweat on her upper lip. She grips the arms of her chair so hard she's splintered the wood.

"Please, sit there," Moab requests, pointing to the chair just beside Alivia. "And give the viewers a little smile."

I sit in the chair he indicated, but I certainly don't give the camera a damn smile.

"Sevan, this is Jersey Adams," Moab says, shifting his green eyes from me to the blonde woman across from me. "She's a news journalist from the country I hear you were reborn in. America. When I contacted her, she jumped at the story, but I don't think she quite knew what she was getting herself into."

He gives a little laugh, deep and dark. He smiles, looking her over appreciatively.

Of course. The second he says her name, I know exactly who she is. She's one of the most popular journalists on one of the most popular national news channels.

Jersey Adams looks terrified. She's stark white. She sits still as a statue. I'm pretty sure she's going to be sick at any moment.

"Jersey, I'd like to introduce you to the legend herself," Moab continues, sitting up straight. He's in the camera's sight, it's focused to fit the three of us in the frame. "All these stories we've told you, and this is the woman who was there to witness all of it. The resurrecting Queen herself, Sevan."

Jersey swallows once, and I can see fear all over her face and smell it on every inch of her. "It's...a pleasure to meet you. The stories I've heard...they're quite incredible."

I don't say anything. I haven't gathered enough information, I don't know what they all know yet. I need to wait and gather more intel before I make a move.

Or try to murder Moab in front of possibly millions of viewers.

Shit.

My organs are gone. Ash.

This really is it. The end.

The whole world will know now.

Come morning, the time for quiet and secrecy will be over.

"It has been a very, very educational hour," Moab continues. He leans forward, resting one elbow on the table, pressing two knuckles to his chin. "The interviews are fascinating. Hearing everyone's take on our history..." He shakes his head and smiles. "It has been enlightening to see how different individuals paint the history."

Moab sits forward, and my stomach does a jolt when he reaches forward and takes a lock of Alivia's hair in his fingers, twirling it back and forth. He studies her, his eyes trailing up and down her neck.

I don't love Alivia. Not yet.

But I want to pluck every one of his fingers from his hands as he touches her.

I want to peel his flesh from his body and turn him inside out.

Alivia sits there, breathing hard, her nostrils flaring.

But she's frozen. Staring right at the camera.

"Your mother..." he suddenly stops speaking and looks directly at the camera. "Yes, they may look the same age, or within a few years, but this woman," he turns back to Alivia, I swear, eye raping her as he continues to play with her hair, "is biologically Sevan's mother."

Moab's eyes flick back up to mine. "As I was saying. Alivia was granting us a very, very interesting interview concerning the Bitten. How they're made. The Debt of slavery to their creators. How they nearly overran her region. And how the King ordered the extermination of their entire kind. How many of them would you say he had killed, throughout the world, Sevan?" He nails me to my seat with his dark gaze. "How many deaths is your husband responsible for?"

"You're very proud of yourself, aren't you, Moab?" I seethe between my teeth. "After all these years, you're finally accomplishing your goal of ruining the world."

"After all these years, I'm finally executing my father's vision," Moab says calmly. He drops Alivia's hair finally and sits back in his seat, locking me with his molten hot vision. "A vision you and my grandfather could never comprehend."

"The lack of foresight was not on our part," I counter. "But congratulations. It only took you two thousand years to accomplish it."

I can tell that hit the mark. Moab's mouth snaps shut.

I look away from him, and my eyes lock directly on the camera.

For a very long moment, I just stare at it.

I've said too much already. I don't know what Javier of the House of Badillo already said in his interview. I don't know what Yuuto of the House of Himura said before Moab killed him.

But after this much coverage…the truth is out there now. The damage has been done. Our world will never look the same.

"I know some of *us* are watching this, or will watch it later," I say. My throat is tight. The words don't come out easily. I have to fight for each one of them.

In the background, I hear something slam into the huge and solid wood door. Larkin attempts to break it down.

"It was never supposed to come to this," I say to the camera, shaking my head. "I've lived in the world where others knew what I was, what my husband was. People who are different, until the world understands them, are feared. And fear makes people do violent things."

I shake my head again, fighting the sting at the back of my eyes. I can't cry. Not now.

"I know this may seem like an exciting, new time," I continue. "But unless you have had to run, unless you have been hunted, you cannot understand. And if you do not understand, do not go trying to change the world."

I can't fight it any longer. Tears well in my eyes as I imagine it in my head. When the most powerful governments in the world realize the truth. When they get ahold of us, when they rip our bodies apart, when they see our supernatural strength, and when they realize that we must feed on their blood to survive. When the powerful confirm the truth, I can see it: how we will have to run and hide. Or how we will fight for our survival against the entire human race.

"I beg you to lay low," I say, my voice little more than a whisper. "I beg you to try to repair the damage done. Don't let it escalate."

Beneath the table, I feel Alivia reach for my hand and squeeze it tight in support.

"After all these years, you still hide in fear?"

Moab sits forward, resting his forearms on the table, glowering at me. His dark green eyes spark with red embers. "With everything we are capable of, with everything you can do. With all the numbers we now possess, you still wish for them all to hide?"

I look away from him. I fix my eyes on a tapestry that hangs from the wall across from me.

There's nothing, absolutely nothing I can say that will make a difference to Moab.

"I truly do not understand how you and your husband remained in power this entire time, when the both of you have lived in such fear," Moab seethes. I feel it. A monologue coming on. We're in for a long speech. "The world does not respect cowards."

There's an even louder whack at the door, and I hear wood splinter. Moab's guards at the door stand in front of it, their swords held at the ready.

Moab hasn't stopped talking, though. He continues his speech. Ranting on and on.

There's another crack against the wood, and a two-foot

long splinter goes sailing across the room, narrowly missing one of the guards.

I tighten my grip around the sword.

I look at the camera.

Can I do it?

Can I take advantage of his distraction and kill him on live TV? Because I know there are people watching. I know millions will see it.

Can I slaughter him in front of the camera?

There's another shattering boom, and I hear the air rush as it sucks into the Hall.

Moab shoots to his feet, drawing his sword, watching the door.

I don't see anyone. But someone tosses some kind of... device inside. It hits the stone floor with a metallic tinkle. My stomach drops when there's a beep, followed by three others.

And then it explodes.

Not with fire and shrapnel.

Gas.

It billows out of the device, filling the air, filling the hall at rapid speed.

It has a faint green hue to it, and the air instantly has the smell of toxic fumes.

Two seconds after it detonates, the very last person I ever expected climbs through the destroyed door.

"Eli?" I gasp, sucking in a breath, trying not to breathe.

His eyes lock on mine, wide and wild.

But my gaze shifts to the two others who crawl through the door immediately behind him.

Larkin slaughters one of the guards, instantly followed by Cyrus, who takes out the other.

A cough draws my eyes back toward the situation I'd found myself in.

Moab has one hand drawn to his throat, and he coughs again. His eyes are confused, angry. He coughs once more, as if trying to clear his throat. He shakes his head, like he's trying to shake it off. With an angry growl, he grabs Alivia by the arm, yanking her into his chest, and presses his sword against her throat.

"Cy…" he growls, but it sounds wheezy, like he can hardly breathe. "Cyrus." He glares death at my fiancé, even as I see a strange, greenish vein rise from the collar of his shirt, stretching up his neck.

"Moab," Cyrus glowers as he steps forward, his sword at the ready. "It's been some time."

Moab coughs again, and Alivia cringes as he coughs all over her. She has a tight grip on his arm, fighting against his grasp. "I had hoped to end this between us, once and for all," Moab says. His voice grows rougher by the moment. There are now green veins stretching out onto his hands, more climbing his neck to his jaw. "But it seems I'll just have to lock you deep in a hole somewhere, and let you starve into agony."

Cyrus smiles, and oh, if it isn't the most wicked thing I've ever seen. "Oh, you may speak all the threatening words you like, my wayward grandson. But you barely look able to stand, much less attempt to take me to a dark prison."

Moab coughs again, and I see his hand holding the sword to Alivia's throat tremble.

I take a breath, testing the air.

It tastes bad. Like there's too much cleaner in the room.

But my lungs don't burn.

I dare a glance down at my arms. I don't see any toxic-looking veins rising to the surface.

As I look around, everyone else looks fine, too. Whatever that chemical was, it only seems to be affecting Moab.

His breathing now comes in struggling pulls, wheezing and gasping. Alivia yanks his arm away from her, doing a twist and turn, yanking the sword from his hands. She takes four steps away, pointing the blade back at him.

Moab looks up with confused, panicked eyes.

It's the first time that I notice Jersey Adams has turned the camera, making sure to capture whatever is happening to Moab. She watches with wide, fearful eyes, but there's a little gleam in them. She's uncovered the most groundbreaking story in the history of the planet Earth.

Moab makes a hacking cough, and drops to his knees. He spits on the floor, and it's mostly blood.

"I have a very dear friend who lives in the charming city of Boston," Cyrus says as he takes a casual step forward, the tip of his sword dragging lightly against the stone floor. "She's a fascinating person. Utterly human. Calm and composed as a butterfly. But she has these skills. She understands chemistry like no one I have ever met before."

Elle.

My eyes widen as it all begins to make sense.

I've heard stories about Ian Ward's little sister. The woman currently taking guardianship of my little brother.

She has a degree in botany and chemistry. She's made things specific to vampires before.

Looking over at Rath, I understand. He and Alivia took forever in arriving to aide because they had to make a side trip to Boston.

For some very specific chemical warfare.

"She's made many fascinating creations before," Cyrus continues as he closes the distance between him and Moab, who is on his hands and knees, gasping for breath. His entire body is covered in those toxic green veins, his body looking as if it's bulging, about to explode. "She can even target specific DNA," Cyrus says as he stops right in front of Moab. "There are genetic differences between vampires and humans. And she even managed to design it to recognize my DNA, Sevan's DNA, and the DNA of any descendants of Dorian or Malachi. But any foreign DNA? Anyone outside of those specific bloodlines?"

Cyrus makes a *tsk* sound. I watch him carefully, noting his relaxed shoulders. The grip he has on his sword. His pursed lips.

I know what is about to happen.

What I don't expect is the sound of a distant explosion. It comes from the direction of the canyon. But Cyrus does not seem worried.

"That is the sound of all your soldiers dying this same painful death," Cyrus says, his voice low and intimate. He goes down on one knee beside Moab, who glares death up at the King. Even his eyes are stained now with that sick green color. "Every one of your soldiers within the castle is now lying on the floor, wondering why they ever thought they could betray a system that has been in place for two thousand years."

Cyrus reaches forward, cupping Moab's face. Almost like a father looking into his son's eyes.

But even though Cyrus loved our son fiercely, even until the day he killed him, that love was tainted by action. Cyrus never found it in him to love anyone ever again, save me.

Cyrus does not love his grandson.

"I have a very good relationship with this incredibly talented chemist," Cyrus says, his voice clear and steady. "We have more, and I know she will provide us with more once we run out, if it means taking care of the issues you have caused. You may have shifted the landscape forever, Moab," Cyrus says as he straightens, standing. "But I am still King."

With a quick, clean motion, Cyrus swings his sword.

Moab's head hits the floor with a small crack. The rest of his body collapses to the ground a moment later.

A tear breaks free and streaks down my face.

I can't identify the exact reason I'm crying. There are a lot of big reasons. All the emotions and fears and the anger I've been feeling for days and weeks, months and lifetimes, pushes out that one tear.

Cyrus turns and looks back at me.

Relief.

I see it there in every inch of his stature.

Moab has been a threat to us since the dawn of our time. Always there in the back of Cyrus' mind.

And now he's finally dead.

I drop my sword and walk to Cyrus, as more emotions bubble up inside me.

Pain. Fear. Grief.

Cyrus lets his own sword fall to the ground and he gathers me up in his arms, pulling me tight to his chest.

I can't hold it anymore.

I cry.

I sob.

I let it all go, finally.

This isn't over. We may have defeated Moab. But Lorenzo Saint Claire swore to kill me.

Moab is dead. His soldiers are dead.

It's a victory. A battle won.

But, I'm just so tired of war.

So I cling to Cyrus, and I let it all out.

CHAPTER 13

It's proof of the number of lives lost and the exhaustion of war.

Somehow Cyrus negotiates a forty-eight hour stalemate with Lorenzo. Forty-eight hours of peace. A tiny reprieve until we all once more pick up our swords and race to end lives again.

We take a count. There were forty-four Royals who came to aide the crown. Only twenty-five survived Moab's surprise attack. Nineteen died. Are gone. Their Houses will be thrown into chaos.

Forty-three Court members were killed up the canyon. Our numbers are so severely diminished.

We can only hope that Lorenzo suffered as many losses as we did, if not more, considering his children were not well trained for war.

I find myself hovering in the doorway of the Great Hall

and the hallway as Cyrus works with Dorian and Malachi, taking stock and making plans.

My gaze is unfocused. My body feels light and numb.

My brain has numbed everything out.

So I jump when a soft hand comes to my back. My eyes dart to find Cyrus, his expression concerned.

"Come, *im yndmisht srtov*," he says quietly as he takes my hand. "We must rest. Everything else can wait until the sun sets again."

I feel guilty. There's so much to do. So much that I know needs to be done. Even as we turn and head for the stairs, I see bloodied and wounded Court members and Royals working to clean out the bodies from the castle.

But I just can't help them.

I'm empty.

I'm so, so tired.

So I let Cyrus take me by the hand and lead me to the stairs. I take advantage of the fact that he is King and I am Queen and that these people serve us as such.

We rise up to the top floor, and my chest loosens just a little when I see our door down the hall. I breathe just a little easier as we get closer, and the tightness releases from my shoulders when Cyrus pulls the door open.

I go straight to the bathroom and start the shower, turning the water as hot as it will go. Without even bothering to close the door or consider what Cyrus might be seeing, I strip my blood stained clothes off, letting them slop into the grand bathtub so the blood doesn't get everywhere, and slip into the shower.

It feels like it takes two lifetimes to wash all the blood off of myself. It's stuck in my nail beds. It's in my ears. It's caked into my hair. My wounds have closed up and healed by now. But I slaughtered dozens today, and their blood soaked me down to the bone.

With my skin bright pink, shiny and clean, I turn the water off, wrap a towel around myself, and step out of the bathroom. Cyrus presses a gentle kiss to the side of my head as I let him by to go shower.

I find a white nightgown on the bed, a soft and shimmery thing Cyrus laid out. It has narrow straps, hugging my bust, cinching under my waist, before flowing down to my knees in pleated soft, sheer fabric.

It feels like heaven.

Ten minutes later, I hear the shower turn off once more, and another minute later, Cyrus walks out of the bathroom wearing soft white linen sleeping pants.

I watch him as he runs a towel over his hair. And I nearly laugh, but I'm too tired.

It's insane. Just a few hours ago, we were both fighting for the lives of our kind, our family of vampires. Being broadcasted to the world and having a secret we've kept hidden for thousands of years exposed.

But here we are. Me in bed, him drying his hair after a shower.

"Come here," I say softly, shifting on the bed so I'm lying flat, my head supported by the pillow.

It isn't just heat that alights his eyes. That's love. Devotion. Caring.

They're all there when he steps forward. They tone his shoulders as he braces his hands on the edge of the bed and crawls up. He balances with a knee between my legs as he climbs up. He settles his weight on top of me. Balancing his elbows on the bed, he holds up something that gleams in the dark room.

My engagement ring.

I'd taken it off in the bathroom. I don't even remember what day that was now, they've all blended into a wash of chaos. I didn't want it to get ruined or lost.

Cyrus takes my left hand and slips the ring onto my finger. He closes his eyes, pressing a kiss to the area in general.

There's so much reverence on his face. And so much exhaustion.

I wrap my arms around his bare back, and he lays his cheek down on my chest.

We're both quiet. No words are spoken, because we're both just tired and exhausted and beaten for the moment.

It's such a familiar position. The two of us tucked together tight. Arms and cheeks and legs pressed together.

But...

A little voice in the far back part of my brain says, no, this isn't that familiar.

I'm nine different people.

But as I think about it right now, I realize—I am Sevan. I've been no one but Sevan for days now. Maybe weeks.

I'm the woman who walked through the marketplace two thousand years ago. The woman betrothed to a terrible man. I'm the one who chose a man no one believed in. I'm a woman who was turned against her will, and somehow found it in her to forgive that man.

I'm a woman who formed a kingdom. Who ruled.

I am Sevan.

My chest tightens. Antoinette. Edith. Shaku. La'ei.

They all begin to blur eventually. I would start to lose them. And I would return to Sevan.

I don't want to lose Logan.

I need her strength. I need her fire.

And Cyrus loves her.

He loves her.

Emotion pricks my eyes. I'm a tangled web of emotions. I know Logan is me and I am Logan. But it stings, knowing Cyrus could fall in love with someone else. And I also rejoice over that knowledge. Cyrus let his heart open again. He found the hole in his heart and filled it.

Cyrus loves Logan.

And despite everything Cyrus is, despite being a difficult person, Logan fell in love with him.

I died for him, a voice in the back of my head says.

And I let myself fall back into that memory. Of days back in Colorado. When I was a mortician's apprentice. When I spent my days in the basement of the mortuary taking care of the dead.

And then it all changed when Eli and I came across a scene we were never meant to see. It all went sideways when Edmond Valdez recognized my mother in my face. When he knew Eli was actually Rath and that he served the House of Conrath.

And then there was Cyrus. He tested my blood and knew I was Royal through both lines.

Our bargain.

I was desperate to live. To find a way to change his mind. I wasn't ready to die. So I told him he had to get to know me for a month.

A month filled with secrets. A month of close watching. Side looks. A month where I began to see the broken and lonely man that was in Cyrus. A month where he took care of me as a woman, a human being. Where we saved each other.

And then I gave it all up to try to save his life. I didn't know that Cyrus was truly immortal. I didn't know the assailants were actually there for me, to try to get to the King.

I just gave up my life so he could live.

Because over the course of our month together, I had fallen in love with Cyrus.

I *am* in love with Cyrus.

He gets my acid. He knows my shit. He pushes me to my limits and pulls me back in with those wicked lips and possessive hands.

I'll hold on to this man until my last damn breath.

My hands fist into his hair, and he must feel my shift. He raises his head, his eyes turning from exhaustion to desire in the space of one second. He shifts forward, and one of my hands cups his face, just before he claims my lips.

A little groan pushes past my own as his right hand comes to my waist and roughly grabs my hip, puckering the fabric there. It slowly works its way around to my back, possessively pulling me into him.

I part my lips, letting his tongue inside of my mouth. It doesn't hesitate.

Greedily, my fingers work their way down from his hair, to his back. I take my time feeling each muscle in his shoulders. His back. The rises and valleys. I find the scars on his skin and the evidence of the wars he's fought in.

Instinctually, my left leg wraps around his waist, and he lowers himself further, grinding his hips against mine.

Oh shit, that's amazing.

"Cyrus," I moan against his neck. My eyes close, my head falling back as he works his way from my lips, down over my jaw, to my neck. He finds my favorite spot, just below my earlobe. But he doesn't stay long.

"Logan," he pants as he continues kissing his way across the front of my chest. And lower, lower, until his lips are between my breasts. He sucks there, and every nerve in my body goes haywire.

I want to claw my clothes off. This thin little fabric is just too damn much. But Cyrus reaches up, taking both my wrists in his hand, and pins them to the headboard. Rhythmically, he kisses his way back up my chest, back to my throat.

I love this moment. I love this bed. I love his skin and my skin and I love them together.

I love this man.

"Be my wife," Cyrus groans into my mouth as he takes possession of it once more. He grinds his hips further into mine, and I'm pretty sure my brain has been lost into oblivion. "Be my wife, Logan. Tonight."

He releases my wrists and I reach up to cup either side of

133

his face. I look into his eyes, and there's so much fire in them. But I see the love there. The promises.

"That's all I want," I breathe.

Cyrus never breaks our gaze as he rocks back, onto his knees. He pulls me up to my knees as well. He holds my hands in his, trapped between our bodies, chest to chest.

"It isn't a grand wedding," Cyrus says. "There aren't family members here. There is no aisle for you to walk down. There are no flowers. There wasn't a moment of preparation put into it, or a single dollar spent."

I smile, my heart fluttering. And Cyrus smiles as well.

"But a marriage isn't any of those things," he breathes. "It's two people who love one another, who vow to never give up on each other. It's you and me Logan. Is it enough for you?"

His last words bring emotions to the back of my eyes. But I'm too damn happy right now. I push them back, and I smile.

I've led a bitter and snarky life since I was in high school. I've had shit luck.

But right here I know I'm the luckiest woman in the world.

"It's enough, Cyrus," I say quietly, reaching up and placing a hand behind his head.

He smiles, and I swear he could melt me and kill me with that smile. I love it so damn much.

"Logan Pierce," he says, and the moment he says my name, my heart breaks out into a fluttering sprint. "I admired your spark since the moment we met, and I respected your determination from the time you drove that bargain." He lets one of his hands slide down to rest in the small of my back.

"And I have loved you since you put me in my place at the House of Valdez. I vow to love you and cherish you and be by your side until the day I take my last breath. I want nothing more than for you to be my wife, and I promise to be the husband you deserve."

The intensity in his eyes makes my knees feel weak. "Will you take me as yours, forever?"

My body feels filled with air, like I could rise up to the sun and never come down. "I do," I breathe. Because he told me once, how he dreamed I would say those words.

He confirms it with the joy in his eyes.

"I thought you were larger than life from the very second I first saw you," I say as my eyes drift down to his mouth. "You turned my life upside down and threw all my plans out the window." I give a small laugh, because all of my plans were so small. "You made my life so much more."

I reach up, touching my fingers to his lips. "I didn't think I should, but I loved you, Cyrus. I love you now, and I'm going to love you forever. Even when I might not look like me."

His expression pales at that and I wish I could take the words back, but they're still utterly true.

"I'm arrogant enough to say that I don't think very many people have loved anyone as much as I love you, Cyrus," I say, grounding us once more, locking our hearts together once more. "I couldn't ever, ever love anyone else after you. I don't ever want to. I'm yours and you're mine. For forever. Do you take me as your wife?"

I could fall into those eyes. They're bottomless. They

contain the infinities. I could swim in stars in them for the rest of my immortal life.

"I do," he says.

From the drawer of my bedside table, I retrieve the ring I got for him. I wish I'd had time to get or make something more meaningful. This is just a simple ring from our treasury, something I think might have been stolen from a kingdom across the sea.

I slip the simple black band onto his finger.

And then neither of us waits for half a second more.

Our lips meet, and this kiss is entirely different. Husband and wife. Partners. Bonded. Man and woman. Lovers.

His hands are greedy and searching. They go to my hips, gripping the delicate white fabric roughly. He uses it to pull my body to his, pressing our bodies together as one. He pulls up, and I'm nervous but excited as he raises the nightgown up and up, until he lifts it over my head.

He takes a moment to look at me, naked and exposed in front of him.

But he doesn't immediately push me to the bed to make love to me for the first time.

He raises his hand to my cheek, his other resting low, low on my back. He stares into my eyes. I get lost in his.

"For however long we have, and for forever after that," he breathes against my lips as he comes close, so close. But he doesn't kiss me. He just speaks his words against my flesh, soft and delicate. "I will love you, Logan."

"I love you," I whisper.

And gently, he wraps his hand around my back. He leans me back, carefully balancing the both of us as he lowers us.

My hands go to the tie of his pants and I loosen them. I shove them down, and Cyrus lowers himself down to meet me on the bed.

And as my head falls back and my eyes roll to the back of my head, I know forever is never going to be long enough with Cyrus.

CHAPTER 14

ALL I WANT IS TO LIE HERE IN BED WITH CYRUS FOR THE next decade. I want to cuddle, and make love, and forget the rest of the world exists.

A honeymoon would be nice.

But just as evening begins to descend, my phone dings. I ignore it, rolling over to tuck myself into Cyrus' chest. He lays an arm over me, gently pressing a kiss into my hair.

Then the phone dings again. And another shortly after.

"I thought that thing was dead, or lost," I grumble, rolling over. A cell phone has been the least of my worries. And who the hell would be contacting me anymore? My life inside that thing is well over.

I grab it from the nightstand, where I haven't touched it in probably a week. It shows three new text messages.

One from Eshan.

One from Amelia.

And one from Emmanuel.

Oh shit.

My brother, my human best friend, and my former boss.

"What is it?" Cyrus asks, laying an arm across my bare stomach and pressing his forehead into my side.

I ignore him, opening the first message, the one from my brother.

So, the news is out. Cyrus is freaking terrifying. The world is kind of a confused and panicking place right now.

"Shit," I let the word slip out.

I open the message from Amelia.

WHAT IN THE EVER BLOODY LIVING HELL, LO?!?! Are you...when...I don't even have words. I saw the news story, it's all over everything. When did this happen? I'm so confused. When did you become a QUEEN? And who the hell is Sevan?

Oh, this is bad. This is really, really, really bad.

Emmanuel's message is simple.

How long have you been a vampire?

"Logan?" Cyrus questions, rising up onto his elbow, looking at me with concern. "Tell me what is wrong."

My eyes fix on a point on the wall across from us. My brain can't quite grasp a direction, any logic. So it chooses numb generalness.

"It's out there," I say. I hand him my phone. "The world knows."

He takes a minute to read through each of the three messages. He eventually sets it down in my lap, and I hear him breathe through his nose, hard, but controlled. Then, without a word, he climbs out of the bed and goes to the closet.

I hardly even get to enjoy the view of his naked ass.

I understand his silence. What is there to say? We can't change it now. It's too late. The damage is done.

I put on clothes, black and sleek and comfortable, just in case Lorenzo decides to go against his end of the bargain. I braid my hair over one shoulder. And then we leave the sanctuary of our bedroom.

On our way to wherever we're going to handle the insanity of this day, I text back. First to Eshan: *Lay low. Don't mention anything to anyone. No one there in Boston knows me or that I'm your sister, so just lay low with Elle and Lexington.*

Next I move to Amelia. I have no idea what to say. How do you tell your best friend that yeah, you're a vampire queen, but you had no idea until three months ago.

I don't know how to begin to explain, I text. *Just know I had no idea about any of this until a few months ago. When things settle down, I promise to give you some real explanations. But all this crazy shit? Take it seriously. Be careful. Be safe.*

It's not enough. But it's the best I can do right now.

Lastly, I respond to Emmanuel. *Only since after my last day. I promise, that's not why I worked for you. Take all these crazy stories seriously. Keep yourself safe, please.*

I don't promise him more of an explanation. It will all be coming out soon. I can only tell him that: to be careful and safe.

It's over. The entire world and the way things once looked, they're over.

The world is totally changed now.

Cyrus and I aim for his office, and find the doors to it open, with plenty of bodies already inside.

"How far has the news spread?" Cyrus demands, walking past everyone and going straight to his desk. He doesn't sit, though. He braces his hands on the desk, looking out at everyone gathered.

Alivia and Rath. Dorian and Malachi. Edmond and Horatio Valdez. A handful from the House of Himura.

"Jersey Adams put together this whole piece," Alivia starts. "It was an hour long special."

My blood goes cold at that. Not just a five-minute news highlight. An entire hour-long story.

"It was aired around the world," Rath continues the bad news. "It's only been out for hours, but they're already saying it's the most watched news report, or TV program ever."

I swear under my breath.

We let Jersey Adams go after that nightmarish night. I'm not one for death and violence. But we shouldn't have. We should have taken her prisoner. Or killed her. Or at the very least destroyed every bit of footage she got.

"My House says things are pretty ugly and chaotic back home," Alivia says, her hazel eyes rising up to meet mine, and then Cyrus'. "Everyone is scared. Our town already had suspicions, a lot already knew. But they've got everyone at my House nervous enough they're holing up at the plantation."

"The country of Russia has enabled investigation teams and an army already," Dorian says. He's pale. He looks sick.

"I've ordered my Houses to go to the safe houses. They're on lockdown until I give them word."

My stomach is in knots.

We aren't fighting.

We can't fight.

We're hiding.

We're hoping not to be eliminated.

Damn Lorenzo. Damn Moab.

"The House of Himura is readying themselves," Noriko Himura says. "We won't go out to fight, but we will defend ourselves if we must."

"Shit," I breathe under my breath.

Cyrus takes five deep breaths through his nose. His hands have curled into fists, his fingernails dug deep into the surface of the wood of his desk.

Suddenly, he pounds a fist on the desk, cracking the wood, but I'll never know what he was going to say or do, because just then, two bodies storm through the doors.

One, a Court member, the other, a man with golden-jade colored eyes.

Everyone is instantly on their feet, stakes and swords pointed in his direction, fangs bared, eyes brilliant red.

But the Court member has him bound with chains, a sword already at his back, and the man is cooperating.

"Explain," I demand, taking two steps forward, holding a short blade in front of me, ready to drive it into the man's heart.

The Court member, who I think is named Cleo, blinks, looking around at us. "He came to the gates this evening," she says. "He says he wants to help us."

I raise my chin, taking another step forward. "And why should we believe you?" I ask. "Why would we believe you are not a spy?"

He reaches into his pockets, and pulls something out. He drops them to the floor, which they hit with a wet smack.

My stomach instantly turns, and I raise a hand to cover my mouth.

Eyes. They're eyes.

Golden-jade colored eyes. Three pairs of them.

"Because I took out his right-hand helpers," he says, staring deadpan into my eyes. "My full-blooded siblings."

I look up at him and Cyrus takes a step forward, his grip tight on his sword.

"There were four of us that lived here at Court," the man continues. "Our entire lives. We were born here, raised here, attended parties here, and made friends here. But here they are. My brother Felix," he says, indicating one pair of eyes. "And my sisters, Lotta and Elisa."

"You betrayed them?" Cyrus asks, his voice tentative and distrustful.

"No," the man says, standing straighter. "They betrayed us. Our kind. They embraced that madman and laughed with him while they planned all of this. And now they're going to get every one of us killed. I know they're not the ones to put an end to this madness, but I thought it was a start."

I study this man, this man who shares the same father as me.

He doesn't look like the others. Where Lorenzo's features are darker, more Italian looking, this man has dark blond, curly hair. It's a little longer, shaggy almost. His jaw is square and strong. He's larger than Lorenzo in stature. He looks strong, capable. He looks almost nothing like Lorenzo, except for those eyes.

The same as my eyes.

"What is your name?" Cyrus asks. He stands beside me, his sword held casually at the ready by his side.

"Maksim," he responds. His eyes slide over to mine, and there's this strange tingle that shoots up my spine.

For the first time, I feel something.

I've had a brother for the last sixteen years and I love him almost more than anything. I'd lay down my life for him.

But this man…I feel this weird sensation.

He's blood.

We share half of our DNA.

He is my brother.

"You understand what's happening in the world right now?" I ask, taking one more step forward.

Everyone in the room shifts a little closer. I am their queen after all, and I am very nearly within striking distance from this man we thought was our enemy.

"It's falling into ruin," Maksim says. He fixes me with those yellow-green eyes.

"How do I know you aren't just afraid?" I ask. "If you are just panicking, realizing I was right all along, you are no good to me, to us. I have no need for cowardly backstabbers."

Maksim takes half a step forward, holding his chained hands in front of him. All the stabby people around me tighten, raising their weapons. But he seems unbothered.

"My siblings may have idealized the world my father

painted, his vision, but I remained indifferent. I never thought he would actually one day mobilize all of those bastard children he'd created throughout the world. I never thought he would have the balls to make his move."

Maksim folds his arms over his chest. "After six hundred years of waiting inside the nest, I really never thought he would live up to all of his talk."

"And you never thought to warn the Crown?" I accuse him.

He shrugs. "As I said, I was indifferent."

"You keep saying that word, but I don't find it very comforting or convincing," Cyrus growls.

"Call it a wakeup call when my friend in Morocco called me last night and said both of his newly Resurrected children had been hunted down and slaughtered," Maksim says through clenched teeth. "Or when the woman I once loved last century cannot be reached in Greece, and this feeling in my gut tells me she's dead. Or when I turned on the news and saw a story of five us who had been rounded up and peeled apart by an angry mob, on live TV."

A long line of curse words slip through my head, in all the languages I've ever spoken.

It's happening.

It's already happening. What I feared most.

What I told both Moab and Lorenzo would happen if we made our kind public knowledge.

"Is there any chance at reasoning with him?" I ask, my voice going quiet. "Is there a chance we could show Lorenzo what is already happening around the world and he would stop? Would he withdraw from this war and ask his children to stand down?"

I don't like it when I see something darken in Maksim's eyes.

He shakes his head. "Lorenzo thinks we need to finish this war here in Roter Himmel, and once he wins, he plans to immediately turn his efforts to the world. He plans to rally all vampires, Born, Royal, even whatever Bitten he can find, and use them to make a stand. He thinks he can bring a balance. He thinks he can strike peace."

"Idiot," Alivia mutters under her breath, reminding me that there are more than just the three of us in the room.

"Such ego," Malachi says. "This is the world we speak of. This is an earth-moving revelation for the world. And he believes he can smooth it all over?"

"He truly does," Maksim says, looking over at my youngest grandson.

"What are you offering us?" Cyrus asks. His eyes narrow at the golden haired man. "Why are you here?"

Those yellow-green eyes turn to the King he lived under for so long. I see commitment in them. I see devotion. I see resolve.

"I'm here because I don't want to see the world fall into ruin," Maksim answers. "I'm here because I don't hold his beliefs. And I'm here to tell you that Lorenzo plans to attack at noon tomorrow instead of holding to the stalemate."

CHAPTER 15

WITH ONLY TWELVE HOURS TO GO UNTIL LORENZO TRIES TO surprise and slaughter us all, we have six until we will attack, at dawn.

We still have 332 bodies left, between Royals and Court members. And we arm every one of them. Swords, guns, nerve agents, bombs.

I wanted to drop a bomb on them all. But Maksim informed us that after seeing what we had done to Moab's men, they dispersed. They're all holing up in different locations, gearing up and readying for war.

We'd only be guessing as to where to drop the bombs.

If only we had one of Elle's DNA gas bombs. We could set them up all over Austria if it would take them out.

But that would mean I'd die, too. And I'm not about to flee the country and hope that would work. Besides, there just isn't time to have Elle develop that.

So we're right back where we started, thousands of years ago. With swords and shields and blood on the field.

There was once a large population of humans who lived here in Roter Himmel. They farmed, they worked, and the members of Court and the Crown fed off of them, and in exchange for protection, large sums of money, and a generally more exciting existence, they let us drink their blood.

But when all of this insanity started, most of them left. One by one, they fled our city. When the real fighting began, not a single one of them remained.

So for us to feed, to refuel, because part of our curse is that we are dependent upon the blood of humans for survival, we have to hunt them.

I wonder how long it has been for most of them. Since the members of Court, or even most of the Royals had to go and stalk down their humans. So many of them have regulars who let them feed off of them. Or they drink donated, bagged blood.

But this is a new era that looks a lot like the old days.

Some things don't change, though: Cyrus and I cannot risk extra trips outside of the castle right now. So our humans are brought to us, willing donors.

In the Great Hall, the willing woman sits in a chair. I come up behind her. And without even looking into her face, my fangs lengthen, and I sink them into the side of her neck.

It's the best thing I've ever tasted. The wet, coppery fluid slipping down my throat. There was a burn in there that had been eating at my stomach, my esophagus, my tongue. And as her blood slips down, it cools and rewarms and pulls a moan from me.

But I keep drinking.

Even though this is disgusting. Horrifying. I'm draining a woman of her blood.

I have drained blood out of people before. I'd replace it with embalming fluid what would help preserve the body.

But those people had been dead, and I was getting paid to do it as a mortician.

Now I do it for survival.

Cyrus releases the man he drinks from, and quietly waits for me to finish, his human leans back in the chair to recover.

I pull another, and know that I need to stop soon.

But I drink just one more time, because there's a small little flame left in my stomach I haven't put out just yet.

Footsteps from the doorway pull my eyes to the side, and I allow my eyes to follow for just a moment without releasing the woman.

It's Grace Stevens, the human woman Cyrus brought here from New Orleans. The one who is a death detector. The one he forced to give up the rest of her life so she could give us warning if I was going to die soon.

Honestly, I haven't thought about her in weeks. I feel terrible, suddenly. Because neither Cyrus nor I have thought to protect her. We haven't checked on her. I wonder now how she survived when Moab and his people invaded the castle.

How did she survive?

The dark and confused look in her eyes is enough for me to release the human woman. The stiff set to her shoulders is enough to make me stand straight. The way her mouth hangs open just a little is enough to get Cyrus to his feet instantly.

But neither of us says a word. We keep staring at Grace, both of us utterly frozen.

Grace takes a step further into the Great Hall. Her expression doesn't change. She doesn't look scared to have just seen me sucking a human's blood down. She's seen plenty in the last three weeks since she's been here at the castle.

She holds that look of fear and hesitancy.

"Grace," Cyrus finally breathes, as the older woman slowly makes her way across the large space. "What is it?"

My stomach sinks, to that same place where there is a little fire still burning.

Grace's eyes meet mine. And I feel it.

I know it.

"It starts as this…smell," she says, her first words. They come out raspy and quiet. "Like this…cold, misty smell."

Her eyes are locked on mine.

It isn't Cyrus she looks at with those suspicious, fearful eyes. It could and never will be Cyrus she looks at in that way.

"Just faint, barely detectable," she says, taking another two steps forward. "And then it gets stronger. And the bad, oppressive dark feeling starts, and the weight on my chest grows heavier."

I hear it.

Cyrus' heart stops.

He doesn't breathe.

No blood pumps through his veins.

Maybe he can die.

Because everything that qualifies him as living just stops right then.

"I smelled it just a few minutes ago," Grace says, fixing me with her gaze. "It called to me all the way up to the next level. It found me, even that far away."

She reaches forward and takes my right hand between both of hers. She looks so scared, so sad. Emotion wells in her eyes, just slightly.

"It's faint," she says. She lets her eyelids fall shut, and it pushes out two tears, one from each eye. "But there's no mistaking it."

She opens her eyes as she turns her head toward Cyrus. "Death is closely following your wife."

CHAPTER 16

I SWALLOW ONCE.

No.

She's wrong.

I tell myself that there's no fire in my stomach.

I just didn't drink quite enough. I wasn't quite done when she walked in.

"No," I say, shaking my head. "You're wrong. I just...I just need a little more. Watch. See."

I stalk back to the human woman resting in the chair. She has a look of fear in her eyes for a moment that I completely ignore as I grip her shoulders. I sink my fangs into her neck.

And I drink.

Oh, it's so good.

I pull. One deep pull. Another.

I feel the fire in my stomach and it grows smaller. I drink another pull, and the fire dampens a little.

My eyes open, and I stare with wide eyes at the stone floor.

I take another pull. I'm so close to putting out that fire. Just one more. I suck.

I just need one more. I draw again.

So close. My stomach only burns a little.

I pull again.

But nothing comes out.

I snap upright, letting go of the woman. She flops in the chair, hanging awkwardly over the side of it.

No.

My hands raise to my mouth, finding blood on my lips, dripping down my chin.

No.

No.

With eyes wide with horror, I look up at Cyrus.

I killed her.

I drained her dry.

But still there's that little flame in my stomach.

Cyrus is white as a ghost. He stands rooted on the spot, he doesn't breathe. Tears well in his eyes, and his lower lip begins to tremble.

"Cyrus," I breathe, taking a step away from the body. I look down at her and shake my head. "No, I just, I just wasn't paying enough attention. I..."

I look up, my brain stumbling over itself, going a million miles an hour, trying to come up with a solution, anything, to reason why I just did what I did, and why I'm *still* thirsty.

I meet my husband's eyes again. His face breaks, though he tries very hard to keep control over it. He squeezes his eyes closed, bracing his hands on the back of a chair as he collapses forward, barely catching himself.

"No," he whispers, so quiet my ears barely catch the word. He collapses down, dropping to his knees, even as he clings to the back of the chair for dear life. "No. No, no, no."

It breaks me, and I completely forget Grace Stevens is still in the room. I'm at his side in the blink of an eye. I kneel down on the stone floor beside him. I take his hands in mine, but find him limp. I place my hands on his cheeks, forcing him to look at me.

"Cyrus," I breathe. *"Im yndmisht srtov.* Cyrus, I…" But I can't find any words.

I'm supposed to be strong when he is weak. I'm supposed to carry him. Because that is what marriage is—picking up the other when they're down.

But I can't find any strength right now.

"Cyrus," I say as my voice cracks.

He opens his eyes. They're bloodshot. They're broken. Shattered.

He raises his hand to my own cheek, and studies my eyes. He searches deep, probing. He's memorizing, I know it, learning every line and every curve.

He's storing every detail for the time when he won't be able to look at my face again.

He presses his lips to mine. The kiss is gentle, as if I'm instantly fragile. Like I'm about to break. His lips caress mine. They don't move. He breathes a breath in, as if he can suck my soul into him and we can just inhabit the same body instead of mine wasting away before his eyes.

He pulls me into his arms, and he tucks his face into my

neck. And here I can hold him. I can keep him upright. I can support him. I can keep it together as he falls apart in my arms.

I can't believe it. After 286 years apart, we only got three months together. Seventy-nine *days*. Never has our time together been so short. Never have we been so robbed.

It's not fair.

Not fair when this time was so different.

We should have had centuries together.

My shit luck continues, I think to myself.

Of course when I marry the perfect man for me I'd learn within hours that I would die soon. This is just my life. Everything is too good to last.

I lace my fingers through Cyrus' thick hair, letting my eyes close.

Even if I had known from the start that this would be all we'd get, I wouldn't change things. I would still have let myself fall in love with him. I still would have married him last night.

I love you, my heart beats, over and over and over.

Suddenly, Cyrus pulls away and turns back to Grace. "How long?" he demands.

She's pinned to the spot by his smoldering gaze. He's the ultimate predator and every nerve in her body knows it right now.

"I never know exactly," she says. And to her credit, her voice does not tremble in fear. "But once I sense it, it's never too long."

Cyrus looks back at me, and we're both thinking the same thing, doing the same mental calculations.

Once the unquenchable thirst starts, I've never had longer than three weeks.

"Once again I have shit timing, don't I?" I say, doing the only thing I can think of right now, trying to lighten the mood. "Deciding to die right as we're about to go to war."

Cyrus shakes his head. I knew he wouldn't think it was funny, but I had to say something. "I'm so sorry, *im yndmisht srtov*," he says, once more bringing his hand up. He brushes his knuckles against my temple, brushing my hair out of the way. "For doing this to you. That you have suffered for my greed, for my ambition, over and over again. I…" his voice cracks and he closes his eyes for just a moment. "I wish I could take it all back."

For a second, I'm scared. I wonder what is wrong. Because his expression suddenly goes blank. His eyes widen. His hand freezes against the side of my head.

I can see it in his eyes, the gears spinning in his head a billion turns per second.

Finally, he takes a deep breath, and I see something spark in his eyes.

"Alivia," he breathes under his breath. He takes my hand, and before I can demand an explanation, he's on his feet, dragging me with him through the Great Hall and out into the hallways.

"Alivia!" he bellows, looking every direction.

"Cyrus," I say, trying to pull him to a stop. But he's determined and focused. With singularity, he follows his ears up to the next floor.

"Alivia!" he yells, his voice filling the entire castle with its power.

Down the hall, I see her step out of a bedroom.

She's terrified. From head to toe, I can read the fear off of her. I can sense her flashbacks of their past, when Cyrus tortured this woman, when he left scars so deep they took sixteen years to heal, and now only two seconds to reemerge.

"Was it true?" Cyrus demands, stopping just three feet from her, his hand still held tightly around mine. I've never seen this kind of focus on Cyrus' face. Such determination. "Did he create it? Was he successful in making a cure?"

More of my internal organs disappear.

Cure?

"Cyrus?" I breathe, fighting through the confusion raging through me like a panicked toddler. "What are you talking about? What cure?"

Alivia's eyes flick from Cyrus' to mine. And I see it there. Written all over her face, over every inch of her body language. She knows something. Something important.

Something life-changing.

"Alivia!" Cyrus bellows when she hesitates in answering. He releases my hand and suddenly grabs her, gripping her upper arms and shaking her. "Did Henry really make a cure?"

"That would be impossible!" she yells. And I see a spark in her eyes. She'll fight back. She yanks back, out of his grasp. She glares at him, stepping out of his reach.

"Don't toy with me, Alivia," Cyrus hisses. He takes a step forward, glaring death and curses at my biological mother. "In this matter, you have never learned your boundaries."

"Cyrus," I scold, stepping forward and grabbing him by the back of his shirt as he stalks forward and Alivia slinks back. "What the hell are you talking about? You're acting like you've lost your damn mind!"

"I am losing my mind!" he shouts, turning, his eyes igniting red as he looks from Alivia to me. "I've only just found you, Logan! I will not lose you. Not this soon. Not ever."

Instantly, Cyrus eyes soften. They break with grief.

"What?" Alivia breathes. "Lo...Logan. What is he talking about?"

I look at her, and in my brain, I open my mouth, and I very clearly explain it.

The curse is coming for me. My time is up. I'm going to start getting sick. I'm going to starve, no matter how much blood I drink. I'm going to wither and die a painful death.

It's simple.

I've done it eight times before.

But my lips don't part. Instead, the bottom one trembles, just a little.

It's answer enough. The entire world knows the story. Alivia knows it.

She understands.

Without a word, she reaches out, grabbing my wrist and Cyrus' and pulls us into her bedroom.

"Come inside," she says before she looks both directions down the hall and then closing the door behind her.

Slowly, she turns around and crosses her arms over her chest.

"What does a cure have anything to do with it?" she asks simply.

I go to the chair in the corner, because suddenly, I am

tired. Maybe it's mental. I pretend there's no way it's physical. Not this fast. Not this soon.

"She cannot die Sevan's cursed vampire death, if she is not a vampire," Cyrus says.

My brain trips. It falls smack on its face, bloody nose gushing, and wonders what the hell just happened.

"I need the both of you to explain what you're talking about," I grit out from between my teeth, looking from Cyrus, to a very guilty-looking Alivia.

"Alivia's father and I were enemies for centuries," Cyrus says, obliging in giving an explanation. "Bad blood over other issues aside, there were rumors about some research Henry Conrath was conducting. Research on me."

My eyes widen at the words, and I look back at Alivia, whose expression darkens. But she doesn't say anything. She just stares at Cyrus.

"He'd taken samples of my DNA without me being aware, and had built a laboratory of sorts for the age, and was studying what made me what I am." Cyrus' grip on my hand tightens and I can feel his hatred, his rage. Cyrus hates this man, my biological grandfather, Henry.

"My spies broke into the lab, analyzed what Henry was working on," Cyrus says. "They were not men of science. But they had their suspicions."

My heart pounds a little faster.

"They did not seem to be complete, however," Cyrus continues. "So I told them to return again in a year and see what became of Henry's experiments. But when they returned, they found that the lab no longer existed and Henry had moved. To America, with his brother Elijah."

This is one of those beautiful and incredible parts about what we are. Our immortality. The time that can pass, and the changes that can happen in those large spans of time.

"We watched Henry for years. As he bounced around New England, and then finally settled in that swamp you call home." A little sneer curls on my husband's lips as he looks at Alivia and recalls the area she rules. "We waited to see if he resumed his studies. But we never found evidence of a lab. So, we came to the conclusion that he had abandoned whatever study of my DNA he had been conducting. And then he was killed, sixteen years ago."

I'd never heard Alivia talk about her father. I knew he had to have died, or he would have been ruling at her side. But here I hear it. The quick summary of his demise.

"But you think he created something?" I say, my voice quiet. I swallow once. The burn in my stomach is a little hotter, a little more present. "You think he made some kind of cure?"

Cyrus does not look away from Alivia. He stares at her like he can see right down to her soul and read the truth off of her blood cells.

"We thought he had created two cures," he says. And when I smell the sweat break out onto Alivia's palms, I see the smile begin to curl on Cyrus' lips, just faintly. "A cure for the Bitten. I have my suspicions he used it on his friend, Rath. The man is neither human or vampire. I think Henry altered him, somehow made him age slower. And then I think he made a cure for any kind of vampirism. Even mine."

Shit.

Shit.

No. No way. Not possible.

Not freaking possible.

"I really did think Henry Conrath was dead," Cyrus says. He takes a step forward, and Alivia takes an equal one backward. "And was relieved for it. But then ten years ago, word of someone curing Bitten circulated back to me, and I remembered my old enemy."

The smell of Alivia's fear doubles.

"You are quite the actress, Alivia, I know this from experience," he says as he drops my hand and takes another step forward. I climb to my feet, ready to pull him off of her at any second.

I'm just waiting for him to pounce.

He's utterly terrifying right now.

"But I know how to put on a face myself," he continues as his voice drops in volume. "Elle told me a beautiful story about how a professor helped her create a cure for the Bitten, but I knew better." Cyrus smiles. And I love his smile, but it is the most frightening thing in the world right now. "I let her think I believed her. But it sparked my doubt. As far as we suspected, Henry hadn't completed his cure for the Bitten, only experimented on Rath. But then I learned the cure had been in use for several years. So either Henry hadn't utilized it for a space of time before his death. Or he never really was dead."

Alivia doesn't say a word. She just stares darkly at Cyrus, as if willing him to stop reading her so easily.

I realize that Cyrus has been quiet for a long moment. I look up at him at the same time he looks back at me. There are emotions beginning to pool in his eyes. His breathing is shallow. He's trembling slightly.

His emotion draws my own out.

I'm not ready.

I don't want to die.

I want to live. I want to live with Cyrus and have a life together.

It's not been enough.

Not even close.

And I'm only twenty years old, damn it!

Cyrus turns back to Alivia. And to my shock, he drops to his knees in front of her.

"I know you hate me," he says. "I know you and your family have every reason to. We've been enemies for so long. But Alivia," he reaches forward, taking one of her hands in his. He presses his forehead to the back of her hand. "I will forget it all. I will erase it all, somehow. Just please tell me. Did Henry succeed in creating a cure?"

Alivia stares down at Cyrus, and I see tears gathering in her own eyes. She's shaking. Like she's holding something in. Like she's not quite strong enough to keep it all.

Her eyes rise, and meet mine.

I feel tears break free from my eyes at the same time they break from hers. We're staring at one another, trapped in this suffocating bubble of fear and uncertainty and secrets and lies. And lives are on the line. Hers. Mine. Henry's, possibly.

The flames jump from my stomach up into my throat, and instinctually, I raise a hand to it, swallowing twice. But it doesn't help.

It cracks her.

I might not love Alivia yet. But maybe she loves me.

Because she closes her eyes, forcing out a whole stream of tears. She covers her mouth with her hand, silently crying for a full minute. Her shoulders shake. Her hand, still in Cyrus', trembles. But not a sound comes from her lips. Her crying is silent.

Just like mine.

I don't want to die.

I don't want Alivia to have to betray her father's secrets.

"He did," she says. "He made it."

I hear the air suck into Cyrus' lungs once more. I feel his relief flood into the room. And it loosens my own lungs. I take a step forward, but I don't know where I'm going or what I was going to do, so I stop, clutching my hands hopefully at my chest.

"Tell me where it is Alivia," Cyrus begs. He presses his lips into the back of her hand, begging. Pleading. "Tell me where it is and I will give you anything in the world you want. Anything."

Alivia's lip continues to tremble, and even more tears streak down her face. Her eyes rise up to meet mine. "I don't know where it is."

Cyrus' head drops. It hangs in defeat, and I feel it, too.

So close.

But we'll never get what we want.

It's part of our curse.

"While I was here a few weeks ago," she continues, to my surprise, "Henry came to the House."

At that, Cyrus' head snaps up.

"He is alive," he says. A statement. Not a question. Not a growl. Just a statement. A hopeful one.

Alivia nods her head. "He went to the House while Ian and I were gone. He had a lab, it was hidden, you'd never, ever find it. And he cleaned it out. When I got home from here, Henry was gone, and everything he'd ever created was gone with him."

"Where did he go?" Cyrus asks with hope as he climbs to his feet, like he's going to run out the door the second Alivia tells him Henry's location.

Alivia shakes her head and shrugs. "I don't know," she admits. "Henry has come and gone the entire time I've known he was still alive. I think in part so you won't ever find him and kill him."

Her dark eyes tell me she isn't happy about that fact.

Alivia never knew her father, had no idea who he was until he was supposedly killed and left his house and estate, and vampire heritage to her. So her time getting to know the man has only been since he was found to not be dead.

"Do you think you would be able to track him down?" Cyrus asks hopefully, ignoring her last statement. "Do you stay in communication with him when he is gone?"

Alivia sighs and turns away from Cyrus, taking a few steps away, as if she's trying to collect herself. And I can't blame her. This was massive, what she just revealed.

The fact that she did isn't lost on me.

"Sometimes," she says. "Sometimes he drops off the face of the planet. Other times he calls every day."

"And this time?" I ask.

She looks back at me. "I haven't heard from him since he took off."

My brain, which has been in war and survival mode for thousands of years begins trying to sort through what his disappearance with all his research means. What he's planning to do with the cure for vampirism, and who knows what else.

But that's not my biggest concern at the moment.

"Do you think you could track him down if you tried?" Cyrus asks. Once more, there's that begging, pleading tone in his voice.

An ember lands in the back of my throat. I try to clear it quietly. But it still sits there, just smoldering, being annoying.

I cough again. Cyrus' head whips back, and I see panic and fear in his eyes. I hold a hand up, trying to reassure him that I'm fine. For now.

"I will try," Alivia says. And her tone has changed. There's urgency in it now. "Give me a few hours to make some phone calls."

Cyrus crosses to my side, wrapping an arm around my waist. "Do whatever it takes. Any resources I have are at your disposal."

Alivia looks at me with wide, sad eyes, and nods.

Cyrus takes my hand and heads for the door. "Let's get you something to drink."

It's only been thirty minutes since I last drank. But I'm already so damn thirsty again.

CHAPTER 17

THERE'S STILL BLOOD ON MY LIPS WHEN DORIAN AND Malachi step into Cyrus' office. There's a human man lying on the couch on the far side of the room, recovering.

I hope he recovers. I took more than I should have. Fingers crossed he doesn't turn into a Bitten.

"Is everyone ready?" Cyrus asks. He sits propped against the ledge of his desk, his arms folded across his chest. There's anticipation in his shoulders, keeping them tight and poised. We're in this stage of waiting, and it's on something that could save my life.

"Yes, my King," Malachi says with a little bow. "They are all armed and ready. We're waiting for your command."

I wipe the blood from my lips, and force myself not to look at the human man. I try to ignore the sound of his beating heart, the whoosh of blood rushing through his veins. It's taking every ounce of self-control I have to not grab him once more and finish draining him of every drop.

The burn has crept from my stomach, all the way up to the base of my throat.

It's hot. And annoying. Like a bad sunburn.

"I tell you this because I trust the two of you second only to my wife," Cyrus says, staring at his grandsons. "Because you have proven your loyalty over and over through the centuries."

"I'm dying again," I speak up.

Cyrus is taking too long. And I need everything to move in fast motion right now, because my moments are limited.

"The thirst has already kicked in," I continue, ignoring the annoyed but sad look Cyrus is giving me right now. "I can feel it, like the other times. I've got a couple weeks at best, and then I'll be gone."

I walk over to Cyrus' side and take his hand in mine. I'm not sure why I do it. I'm scared. But not panicking. He's grieving already, but doing everything he can to stop this.

Maybe I do it just because he's my husband.

Holy shit. I haven't even gotten two seconds to process that yet.

He's my husband.

I'm married.

But I'm about to leave him a widower already.

What a sucky wife I make.

"I can't exactly go onto the battlefield when all I can think about is where I'm going to find my next drink," I continue. Only now do I take note of my grandson's expressions. They're disbelieving. Shocked. Sad. "We need the both of you to lead this last battle."

"Our world is changed, forever," Cyrus says, looking

from our hands held together, up to Dorian and Malachi. "It will never look the same. But we must fight and we must finish this last battle."

They both look from the King, to me, and back to the King. Each of them nods.

"Of course, your majesty," Malachi says, bowing deeply once more.

"Please, tell us if there is anything more we can do," Dorian says. There's so much grief in his eyes. He has always valued family. He is my family, and I am his. Even if he has only known me with this face for five weeks.

"Thank you," I offer.

Cyrus cannot say the words, but he nods the same. He clears his throat once, looking away when I know there are emotions pooling in his eyes. "If everyone is ready, strike now. Every second counts if we can catch them off guard."

"Yes, my King," they say at the same time. They offer one more bow, Dorian gathers the human man I fed from in his arms, and they leave the office.

It's like we're both holding our breath. We wait. Side by side, we listen to the sounds of war. The gathering. The speech. Dorian and Malachi bolstering the Court members and Royals. Maksim giving them important insider information on Lorenzo.

They question our grandsons about where Cyrus and I are.

Dorian answers them honestly. He says that the Queen is not doing well and that the King is attending to me.

They know what that means.

I know that Cyrus did not intend to tell everyone. But this

will make them fight harder. It gives them one more thing to fight for. Grief can weaken people, but it can also motivate them. Drive them to work harder, to fight harder.

And with a simple command, I hear them all leave. Quiet. Stealthy. They must use every moment of surprise to their advantage.

We're alone in the castle, save for twenty guards left behind.

I let out a slow breath. I feel tired. Like I've been stretched too far for too long. And now I've lost all my strength and elasticity.

Cyrus was right. When he'd told me that he was tired of fighting. Over and over. Keeping such a tight grip to keep everyone safe. To keep the world balanced.

Maybe I should have walked away when he asked me to. We could have just slipped away to some remote corner of the world. We wouldn't even have known what became of Roter Himmel and these wars. We wouldn't know of the exposure of our kind. We could have just been normal and happy and removed.

It's a pretty picture. It sounds relaxing.

But in reality, neither of us could have ever done it.

I look down at our hands laced together, only to find that I got blood on my shirt. I think I go into autopilot, because I head toward the door without saying anything. Cyrus follows.

Through the halls and up the stairs I rise. My feet know where they're going, even if my mind isn't paying attention. To the top floor I head, and then down the hall, toward our bedroom.

As soon as I walk through the door, I strip my shirt off and toss it into a corner. It's ruined. It was white, and there was a fairly large amount of blood on it.

I pause in the middle of our room, like I'm not quite sure where I'm going or what I should be doing right now. I think my brain keeps overloading and apparently my default is to zone out. How Queen-like of me.

I hear the door shut, and a moment later, a soft hand slips around my waist, and a pair of lips presses against my bare shoulder. My body relaxes as Cyrus pulls me back against him, and I fit there perfectly, as if we were molded to fit together as one.

"I swear, I won't let it happen this time," Cyrus purrs against my flesh. "This will work."

"Shh," I breathe, reaching a hand up and hooking it behind his neck. I tilt my head to the side, inviting his lips to find my flesh there, and he must be a mind reader, because they do.

I don't want to talk about things I can't control right now, things he can't control.

I want to be here, in this world. I need to be present.

I place my hands over Cyrus' and guide them around me. I nearly moan at the contact. His flesh against mine. I feel his heat. The realness of him.

I turn, never breaking his embrace. My hands go to the hem of his shirt and I slip my hands underneath it. There, I find firm stomach muscles. I find valleys and rises. My hands slide over them, even as my eyes meet Cyrus'.

Our eyes are both brilliant red. Heat radiates off of Cyrus' body in a very real way.

He takes a step forward, pushing me further into the room.

I give a tug at his shirt, ripping it from the bottom, to midway to the collar.

I look up at Cyrus, and he gives a wicked smile.

He liked that.

Not breaking the eye contact, I tug at his shirt again, splitting it clean in half, exposing all of his chest and stomach.

The wicked gleam in his eyes darkens and his nostrils flare a bit.

Oh, he liked that a lot.

I place my hands on his bare chest, appreciating the muscles under all that hot, flushed skin of his.

I want to lick him. I want to devour every bit of him.

So I do. I let my tongue explore all the low places of his torso. My blood lights with electric fire as I run my mouth and my hands down his body and back up. My mouth makes its way to his neck and he moans, gripping my hips possessively.

"Don't stop, Logan," he groans.

I hear it in his voice. He'll die if I stop. His heart would stop and everything would turn to ash.

I love that it's me—me—who does this to him.

I smile wickedly as my fangs graze along his neck, all the tendons and muscles taut. My hands have a mind of their own as they pull the tattered remains from his shoulders and let them fall to the floor.

It may have been his eyes that I first fell in love with. But I love these shoulders. Strong and muscled. But I also love the feel of his back. The way it ripples and shifts as he moves.

Or maybe I love his hips, the ones he lifts me to wrap my legs around.

My back hits a wall, and his hips grind deeper into the center of me. My head falls back, hitting the wall, but I don't care. Not when his tongue is making its way from my breast-bone, up to the hollow beneath my ear.

This. I *married* this.

These hips. That back. Those shoulders. They're mine.

Not just a hookup. Not boyfriend. Not fiancé.

This is my *husband*. I am his wife.

Cyrus slowly lets me slip down him as my hands come to his cheeks, pulling his lips to mine. I kiss him with reverence. I kiss him with every ounce of love I have.

I feel that love from the tips of my toes, all the way to the ends of every strand of hair on my head.

"I love you," I breathe against his lips. "I love you so damn much, Cyrus."

His hands slip around my waist, holding me gentle and firm. It's a promise, this hold. It's the world in its reality. "I love you, Logan."

And I don't feel it, the burn in my throat, I don't feel the weight that's developing in my chest. I just feel Cyrus' skin against mine. He undoes the button of my pants, and I break the one on his.

He carries me to the bed, and whispers love against my skin, over, and over, and over.

CHAPTER 18

My eye squints open. Through the dim light, I can't see anything but gray, hazy shapes.

I roll over and realize I was nose to shoulder with Cyrus. It was his blurry shape granting me a lovely landscape.

I didn't expect to fall asleep, but at some point after making love, I must have, tangled up in Cyrus' arms and legs. Groggily, I push my hair out of my face and look over at Cyrus.

He lies on his back, one arm hooked up behind his head. His hair is utterly insane, sticking up in every direction. One leg is straight, the other crooked up. The covers are lazily thrown over his naked form.

I smile as I look at him. He looks so peaceful. His lips are parted just slightly. His long, dark lashes fan over his cheeks.

He's so damn beautiful.

And he's mine.

My stomach twists with hunger. Careful not to disturb

him, I climb from the bed. I pull on comfortable, simple clothes, and head out of the sanctuary of the bedroom.

The castle is so quiet. I can hear the guards, mostly by the entries to the castle. But they don't say a word. Like they're watching and waiting, poised to fight at one movement in the shadows.

I don't bother them. I silently slip down the second and third floors, and descend into the fourth.

I find the kitchens empty, which is a relief, and also disappointing, since my cooking skills are zero.

I rummage through the massive pantry and then the refrigerator. Here there's evidence of war and turmoil. Our supplies are low. There hasn't been an opportunity to get supplies in weeks, now. There's been no one cooking. There's been no regularity in the entire time since I've returned to Roter Himmel.

It'll never be normal again.

I find a loaf of bread that hasn't gone bad and a jar of peanut butter. After an extensive search in the massive walk-in unit, I find some jars of mulberry jam.

A PB and J sandwich. That kind of cooking I can handle.

I sink into the small eat-in table in the corner of the massive, commercial grade and sized kitchen and bite into the sandwich with a satisfied moan. I even prop my bare feet up on the table, tipping back in my chair.

"I guess even the Court's chefs couldn't teach you how to cook a proper meal."

The voice startles me so badly I nearly tip out of my chair. I must have been really into my sandwich, because I didn't even hear him approaching.

Eli—Rath, Cornelious Rath steps into the kitchen. He folds his arms over his chest and leans against the counter.

And for a second, it's like the old days. Him in the kitchen of my little apartment, making me food so I don't starve. Good friends, just hanging out.

I smile, climbing to my feet. I cross the kitchen in three steps and wrap my arms around his neck, hugging him tight.

Some things are definitely different, though.

I never smelled him before. Never analyzed the smell of his blood before.

He sort of smells tasty. But definitely doesn't.

Rath so isn't human. But he's certainly not a vampire.

Which makes no damn sense.

"I really appreciate you coming," I say, smiling as I look up at him. "Thanks for saving my ass with Moab." I hadn't thanked him yet for barging into the castle with that DNA bomb a few days ago.

"Of course," he says. And he smiles back. He actually does.

Eli doesn't smile often. But when he does, you feel it. You know it's real. You know you're someone special.

"Why don't you sit back down and I'll make you some real food," he says, releasing me.

"It must be my lucky day," I say, finding I'm smiling again. I turn in place and walk back to the table to finish my sandwich.

He just chuckles and sets to taking stock of what ingredients we have on hand.

I let him do his thing. He takes his time going through the

supplies at hand. He grabs this and that. And he starts cooking something up on the stovetop.

"How has it been being back in Mississippi?" I ask.

It feels like forever ago. It really does. When he and I drove to Silent Bend, Mississippi so we could get the cure when Eshan was a Bitten for just a few days. We cured him, and then Eli made the decision to stay at the House of Conrath, where he belonged.

It seems like a whole lifetime ago.

"Strange," he says as he goes about cooking. "My history there is long, but the dynamic is so different. There are a lot of people that live there. Alivia isn't the unsure, untested girl she once was. It's organized and busy and efficient. I don't feel needed there like I once was."

"What do you mean?" I ask.

I want to know. There's so much history to Eli that I never knew about, this whole life he had as Rath that was hidden from me. I want to understand. But he's a man who greatly values his privacy and secrets.

"I used to run the entire estate," he explains, a little to my surprise. "I lived my entire adult life on that plantation. Learned who I was as a man there. Worked there, in many capacities. After Henry was killed, I took care of it, helped Alivia learn how to run things."

"You knew Henry Conrath, then?" I ask in surprise. I struggle to swallow the last bite of my sandwich in my surprise.

Eli looks back at me and nods. "He was my best friend," he says. His tone is dark. There's a hint of...regret in it.

"Was?" I say quietly.

Sharply, Eli's eyes flick back up to mine.

"Alivia told Cyrus and I that he's still alive," I confess. I say the words so quiet. This castle is full of ultra-sonic ears. I won't betray their secret to everyone. "Do you still mean that Henry *was* your best friend?"

Eli turns back to the food, and he doesn't answer me for a good thirty seconds while he considers. "He was. That's just one more way that the House of Conrath is different."

"Is it because he's always leaving?" I probe. I tuck one knee up into my chest, wrapping my arms around it.

He gives a small shrug. "Henry almost never left the estate before his assassination...attempt." The sentence comes out awkward, like he doesn't know how to define what happened to Henry when he was supposedly dead, but wasn't. "I came and went, running the estate's errands. And he and I had a lot of time together. But after he...died, after he came back and we found out he was alive, he wasn't the same."

The food hisses, and it smells amazing as he stirs it in the big pan. "I think death was freeing for Henry. He entirely escaped the world he resented for so long. He didn't want to be a part of the politics and the games. I think he got a taste of anonymity while he was supposedly dead. It never went away after he came back. Henry was my best friend and I will always love him, for who he is and what he did for me." Eli pauses, and I know, there is so much to this story that I will never understand.

"But Henry Conrath is a selfish man," he says. There's resentment in his voice, and I know it's hard on Eli for it to be there. He doesn't look at me when he confesses these words. He stares at the food, every muscle in his body tight. "When he should be at his daughter's side, not only making up for the first twenty-three years of her life that he missed, but guiding her in becoming the leader she needed to be in this world, he's off in the world. None of us know what he's doing. Where he goes. He comes and leaves as he pleases, with no explanations and no promises of when he will return."

It's fascinating how different people perceive others. I see the conflict in Eli when he talks about Henry. Eli knows the good about the man, but the negatives are weighing awfully heavy, tipping the scales.

But when Alivia talks about her father? It hasn't been much that I've heard. But she loves him. *Loves* him. I don't know if she doesn't notice his faults like Eli does, or if they just aren't that important to her, but I know she forgives him always.

I hear it in her voice and see it in her eyes every time.

Almost as if it were on cue, I hear footsteps on the stairs, and I know it's her. Just ten seconds later, she rounds the corner and steps into the kitchen.

She smiles, as if seeing the two of us together does something. Maybe validates her asking him to uproot his life and watch over me for sixteen years. Maybe it's just seeing two family members who have such a deep relationship without her involved.

But she looks happy to see us together.

"Something smells good," she says. "Dinner's on you tonight, Rath?"

He offers a small smile and turns to prepare something else.

"How about some cookies to go along with whatever smells so delicious?" she asks, looking over at me and winking.

My mom. Is making. Me cookies.

So weird.

"You like to cook?" I ask as she digs through the pantry.

"I love baking," she says. "I worked in a bakery for years before I moved to Mississippi. It's actually kind of nice having so many people living in the House, there's always someone to make a treat for."

I smile, imagining her covered in flour, surrounded by her House members, like Christian, and Cameron, and Anna.

I might be her biological daughter, but *they're* her real family. And that's okay.

"So where's Ian?" I ask the question that's been knocking at the back of my brain since I first found her here.

She sighs, measuring out ingredients without even pulling up a recipe. "I made him stay back at the House," she says. "Nial needed some help managing affairs."

Eli—nope, he's Rath when he's around Alivia—looks over at her with this total *dad* look. "That is *not* what happened."

A little laugh huffs over my lips.

This is funny.

Like, really funny.

Eli was always my friend, like an uncle or something.

But he is totally a father figure to Alivia.

"What happened, for real?" I say.

I'm smiling. And it feels good. It's been forever since I smiled.

Alivia glares at Rath, totally annoyed he ratted her out for fibbing the truth. Finally, she gives this sigh and turns back to her work. "Fine. I may have shot him with a nerve agent when he wouldn't agree to stay." She dumps the sugars into the commercial-sized mixer. I laugh, covering my mouth to try and hold it in. It doesn't do much good. She looks over her shoulder and glares at me, trying to suppress a smile. "And then Christian and Nial may have helped me lock him in this well-prison room in the middle of the house. I told Nial not to let Ian out until he agreed to stay home and not try to come after me."

"You're holding your own husband prisoner at your house?" I say, trying really hard not to laugh my head off.

"I couldn't have him follow me here and get tied up in this war!" she defends with a laugh as she dumps a huge brick of butter in with the sugar and turns the mixer on. "He's fought in more than a few battles, plus he was a hunter before he even Resurrected. You wouldn't believe the ego on him. He would have gotten himself killed on the first day of the fight."

"I'll be sure to let him know you had so much confidence in him," Rath says dryly.

"You will not," she says, brandishing a spatula in his direction.

I can't hold it in. I lose it. I hold my stomach, I'm laughing so hard.

It's ridiculous. And funny. And so normal.

I needed this so bad.

Just as the mixer finishes blending all of Alivia's ingredients together, I hear footsteps on the stairs again. A moment later, Cyrus enters the kitchen.

Everyone freezes for a moment, and the light mood instantly pulls tight.

Cyrus looks around the kitchen. At me. At Rath. At Alivia.

"Is that chocolate chip cookie dough?" he asks. His voice sounds very serious, and very deadly.

"Yes," Alivia answers very nervously.

He doesn't look away from her as he reaches into a drawer, digs out a spoon, and very quietly stalks toward her with a spoon.

I think my heart is stopped.

He's staring at her like he could blink and she'd explode with his mind powers.

Never breaking the eye contact, he dips the spoon into the huge mixing bowl, and scoops out a huge mound.

He takes a small nibble. And a small smile curls on his mouth.

"Delicious," he says, still deathly serious.

Alivia hasn't taken a single breath since he walked into the kitchen.

"Cyrus, knock it off, you asshole!" I yell, breaking the quiet. I throw an apron, which was sitting on the table, at him, hitting him in the head.

He instantly laughs, licking a huge chunk off the spoon and turning away from Alivia.

He was so messing with her.

That man and his games.

Physical or mind games, he's always enjoyed them.

Alivia looks at me over his shoulder as he walks toward me. *You really love this maniac?* she mouths.

I can only smile and shrug.

"Who's hungry?" Rath asks, turning the stove off.

182

CHAPTER 19

IF THE WAR IS GOING LIKE I ASSUME IT IS, NO ONE HAS TIME to give us updates. They're all fighting for their lives. So we'll sit here, wondering what is going on. Who is winning. What the fate of the world will be.

But we don't get to worry about that too much, because at about two in the afternoon, Alivia knocks nervously on our bedroom door.

I scramble to grab clothes, rolling off of Cyrus. His eyes widen in panic, pulling the covers over him.

I can't find my pants, or my shirt. I grab the sheet off the bed, wrapping it around myself.

If I'm down to my last days, I'm going to spend every second I can being happy and experiencing bliss. I've waited twenty years to have sex. And now that I have it with the most incredible man on the planet, someone who also happens to be my husband, I'm going to enjoy it. A lot of it.

I wouldn't have opened the door for anyone other than

Alivia today. And only because we are waiting for her to deliver such important news.

"Trust me, I so did not want to knock on this door," Alivia says, blushing hard when I open the door just a bit. She takes note of the fact that I am only wearing a sheet, my hair is a mess, my skin is flushed, and I definitely smell like sex. But she keeps her eyes down, and I can practically smell the embarrassment on her. "But I knew you would want to know the second I got in touch with Henry."

Cyrus joins my side, a blanket wrapped around his waist. He puts his hand on the door, opening it a little wider, standing behind me.

"Where is he?" he instantly asks.

Alivia's eyes flick to Cyrus' naked upper half for just a moment, and I wonder if it's a sight she's seen before. I know they didn't do anything, because Cyrus wouldn't unless he was sure she was Sevan. But I know she also kind of broke Cyrus' heart by making him hope.

"He wouldn't tell me where he is right now," she says. Her face is so red. "But he agreed to meet you somewhere. He'll be on Lanzarote, one of the Canary Islands, by tomorrow morning."

I look up at Cyrus as my heart jumps into my throat with excitement, and fear. "I've always heard of the Canary Islands, but honestly I have no idea where they are."

"Off the coast of Morocco," he answers. He turns from the door and goes straight for the closet. "Get dressed. We'll leave now."

"He'll meet you at this address," Alivia says. Turning back to her, she hands me a paper. "He wants just the two of you coming. No guards, no Court members. He doesn't even want me coming."

"I understand," I say with a nod. I reach forward, taking her hand in mine. "Thank you for everything you've done, Alivia. I can't tell you what all of this," I wave the paper with Henry's address, but really, it's everything—her telling us all her father's secrets when Cyrus could kill him for it, "means to us."

She doesn't say anything, and I can tell by her pale face that she's still afraid that Cyrus will do something to her father, now that he knows Henry is still alive, and that he has a cure that could change everything. She pulls me into a hug. "Of course," she says into my hair. "I know it's not what it would normally be, but you're family."

She releases me and I smile at her. I feel something in me warm. I feel a little lighter when I look at her.

"Come to the airport with us," I say. "You and Rath have done enough here. You have your husband locked up in a well at home." We both laugh at that. "You should go home and be with the rest of your family."

"Are you sure?" she asks, looking at me with uncertainty. "Kinda' seems like you could use all the help you can get around here."

I smile. "We'll manage. You're needed at home."

She nods and turns to go get her things. "Just don't call me back within days of me getting home this time. International travel is a bitch."

I laugh, shaking my head at her. She winks at me, and turns to go get her things.

In twenty minutes, I'm dressed, packed with an overnight

bag, and Cyrus, Alivia, and I make our way up to the heli-tower. The pilot, ever reliable, and thankfully still alive, waits with the engine running.

I take Cyrus' hand when we're in our seats, our luggage stored, and we're buckled in. We both watch, paying careful attention as we rise into the air.

There. Just barely through the trees, just beyond the mouth of the canyon, I see forms. Bodies. I see fighting.

It isn't over. It won't be over for days. Maybe weeks.

Maybe I won't even get to see it resolved. Maybe I'll be dead by then.

OUR PRIVATELY CHARTERED JET LANDS ON LANZAROTE AT just after nine o'clock. We hire a driver who takes us to a beautiful hotel overlooking the ocean. But I can't even enjoy it. My stomach is on fire. My mouth is the driest desert in Africa.

Cyrus watches my back while I hunt down a man lying in an alley. He hardly even stirs when I sink my fangs into his neck.

I should cringe away from him; he smells disgusting and looks like he hasn't showered in about three weeks. But I just need blood. Now. I'm so thirsty I don't even care if he's clean.

I drink and drink. And it literally takes every ounce of strength I have to release him when Cyrus lays a hand on my shoulder.

I let him go, panting hard, looking down at his neck and the two small trails of blood that slip down his neck. My fingers curl into fists so I don't grab him again. Every beat of my heart is screaming *finish. Take it all. You're still thirsty.*

But I don't want to kill him.

I don't want to turn him.

"Come," Cyrus says. He slips his hand into mine. Gently, he pulls me away from the man. I get to my feet. They follow Cyrus, but my eyes stay glued on that man, on where I can see his pulse beating under the skin on his neck.

I don't go back, though. I let Cyrus lead me away.

We make our way back toward the hotel. In the courtyard that looks over the ocean, there's a live band playing. There isn't a singer, they just play upbeat music. There are couples dancing, looking so happy and light and normal.

Gradually, the burn in my body becomes a little easier to ignore. My brain goes back to normal. I can think again. I can feel.

"Come dance with me," I say, tugging Cyrus toward the dance floor.

He smiles, and I love that there's hunger in his eyes. Just like that.

The song is dramatic, like a tango. In this moment, I let myself be Sevan, not Logan, because Logan doesn't know any actual dances, but Sevan has done these kinds of things over and over.

I slip my hand into Cyrus', and his wraps around my back, pulling me in close. I meet his eyes as we slip into the first step, and he burns me with his intensity. He takes a large step backward, and I match him, keeping our bodies touching along every surface possible.

We slip into a dramatic spin, his hands never leaving my

waist, my back, my thigh. We side step and he drops me into a dramatic dip.

I let my head tip back, my hair brushing the ground. Gently, I feel Cyrus lower his head, and then his lips are pressing between my breasts, exposed by the plunging neckline of my dress.

A wicked grin is on my lips as he raises me up. I wrap a hand behind his neck, touching my forehead to his as he takes steps forward, and I match him step for step.

He spins me, pulling me back to his front against him. Wrapping his arms tightly around me, he sways our bodies.

And as the song comes to its crescendo, coming to an end, he spins me once more. I drape backward, easily caught in his arms, and I raise a leg, wrapping it up around his hip.

And the music stops.

Two people clap, and I hear others whisper.

I look to the side, and see a group, a family maybe, whispering, looking at Cyrus and I with questioning and fearful eyes.

The news cast. Jersey Adams very clearly showed mine and Cyrus' faces.

That familiar feeling of fear spikes in my stomach. One I haven't felt since I wore Sevan's skin.

But not everyone recognizes us. Most are clapping. Most hoot and holler.

I straighten, looking around to see all the other dancers and the diners off to the side had cleared the dance floor everyone was watching us.

I blush, waving at their excitement and enjoyment. I'm

embarrassed I hadn't even noticed we were giving a show. But I certainly keep an eye on the family who recognizes us.

The moment I meet their eyes, every single one of them takes off, back toward the hotel.

Cyrus smiles and pulls me into him. He kisses me, gentle for the crowd, but firm for the intensity of the dance we just shared.

Someone calls out to us, and I swear I don't know what language it is, but somehow I understand the words, the translation happening instantly in my head.

The man asks how long we have been married.

Cyrus responds, smooth and perfect, that we are on our honeymoon.

It's not at all true, but still, I blush as the man congratulates us and winks.

My heart is warm and flushed. I feel...happy. Peaceful.

As the music turns to a slower, gentler song, Cyrus wraps his arms around me once more, pulling me in for a slow dance.

I lay my head on his shoulder, placing my hand on his chest.

A little cough works its way up my throat. Only once. That's all I let form. Despite the burn in my throat.

Cyrus' grip on me tightens slightly. I feel his regret as if it's a physical thing.

"If I could go back in time and reverse what I did, I would," he says quietly. "Back to my time in that lab. My studies. I never would have done any of it. I would have stayed working in the fields, sweating, with bleeding fingers every day, so you wouldn't have to go through this, over and over, Sevan."

I remember those early days. The fear of what my husband had become. The confusion. And then when I was what he was. And then the painful death. Over and over.

I don't say anything. I tuck myself tighter into his chest.

"I am eternally grateful that we have had such an extended period of time together. For all the lives and love we have shared. But I would take it all back, our kind, my immortality." He presses his lips into my hair. "I'd undo it all for you."

I stare at the fabric of his shirt, tracing a fingernail down it. My insides are tight. Twisted up. Because even though I forgave him a long time ago, it doesn't take away the fact that he did it.

The pain is still there, deep down. It opens up every time the end comes. It opens up every time I am reborn.

"I am so sorry, Sevan," he whispers. "I love you."

His words. I know they're true. I believe them with everything in me. So I let go of the pain. I reach up, placing my hand behind his neck and look into his eyes. "I know," I breathe. I'm back in a dusty market, saved from a terrible man by a stranger. I'm begging my parents for permission to be with a poor man with a crazy family reputation. I'm running away in the night with the man I love and marrying him in a field beneath a tree. "I love you, too, Cyrus. *Im yndmisht srtov.* Even after all this time."

He tips his head down and kisses me with the very same lips he first kissed me with over two thousand years ago. He holds me with those same hands. He's just as solid and strong and real as the first day I met him.

He's made a million mistakes since then. He's lost his mind and done questionable things. He's killed and punished and been cruel.

But I know he would do anything for me. He would go to the ends of the earth if I asked him. He'd lay down his life for mine if he could.

No one has ever loved another like I love Cyrus. Like Cyrus has loved me.

CHAPTER 20

I SWEAR, THESE STAIRS ARE GOING TO COLLAPSE UNDER OUR weight. They creak and moan and some of them are so rotted I can see right through them.

The address Henry gave to Alivia to give to us is for what I'm guessing is an apartment above a few rundown shops in the heart of town. It's some kind of spice shop, and the smells coming out of it are strong. Very next door to it, beneath the same apartment, is what looks to be a club.

There's a set of wooden stairs that rises from the ground level up the side of the building. It's sagging, and I swear, the whole thing is going to peel off the wall any second.

We wear sunshades against the growing morning light. My throat is on fire. I couldn't stop myself this morning before we got here. I killed a woman.

I didn't want to. But I literally couldn't stop.

I feel full, sloshy. Filled to the brim.

But my throat still burns. Far worse than it was yesterday.

And I don't feel good. I feel...sluggish. I'm tired. I feel like I could take a nap and not wake up for a week.

This is progressing fast.

We reach the top of the rickety stairs and Cyrus knocks on the scarred red door.

My heart is residing somewhere at the back of my throat, which makes it kind of hard to breathe. My palms are sweating. I feel half blind, because all I can focus on and think about is that door and who and what is behind it, and how this could change everything.

But no one comes to the door.

Cyrus knocks again and we wait another minute. We double-check the address on the paper, and sure it's correct, I put my hand on the doorknob. It turns, not locked. With one look back at Cyrus, I push it open.

Cyrus immediately steps around me, and for a second, I panic.

What if this is a set up? What if Henry decided to turn against us? What if we're about to be ambushed?

My husband's knees are bent slightly, the tenseness in his shoulders says he'll snap at any wrong sound. We didn't come armed, per Henry's request, but we'll fight with our bare hands, if needed.

My ears strain, listening for sounds of life.

Faintly, I can hear breathing coming from a back room.

We entered into a large living room. The furnishings are minimal and worn out, but colorful and thoughtfully chosen. There's a rudimentary kitchen along the far wall. Down the hall, I see a few doors branch off.

Silently, we slip through the living area and down the hall.

The first bedroom is empty, as is the bathroom.

But in that last bedroom, we find a figure standing at the window.

If he hears us come up behind him, he doesn't indicate it. He stands with his back to us, and he seems to be staring outside into the growing light.

I don't see evidence of sunshades, so maybe this isn't Henry Conrath, because if it was, surely he'd be in pain.

With furrowed brows, Cyrus steps forward. Cautiously, he walks up around the man's side, searching for his face. I step forward, and realize I'm holding my breath.

The man I see has nearly shoulder length hair, scruffy, but somewhat kempt. His jaw holds a week's worth of facial growth. His clothes are clean, a suit that looks well worn.

If this is Henry Conrath, he is not what I pictured.

"Henry," Cyrus finally says. He studies the strange man with intense focus and confusion.

There's a view of the ocean from here, beautiful and blue. He just stares. His eyes are filled with sadness. Regret.

"You tried to stop it?" he finally says. "All of this madness taking over the world. You tried to stop it, right?"

Cyrus looks over at me. I see the frustration in his eyes. We came here for a specific purpose, and Henry is acting... odd. I don't know the man, but I do know he's being weird.

"Of course," I answer his question. "We've lost a lot of lives trying to stop it. We're still fighting against it. We left the battle in Dorian and Malachi's hands to come here."

Henry continues staring out into the daylight like it isn't bothering him at all. He nods.

"I stayed out of the game for such a long time, stayed so removed, that I began to forget that there were any others like us out there besides myself and those who are members of my daughter's House. And then the world explodes and now we are everywhere, coming out or being dragged out of the shadows."

I understand that far off look in his eyes now. He's seen something. Maybe he's been fighting some kind of battle. I don't know whose side he's on, or why he took his cures from his lab in Mississippi and disappeared. But Henry has been up to things. He's witnessed things he didn't ever want to see happen.

"I tried to warn them," I say. I step forward, stopping at his side, and I look out over the ocean with him. I'm only able to do so because I still wear my sunshades. "Maybe I should have done more. I should have found a way to tell every single one of them. That we're too few. That there are so many more humans out there than there are Born or Royal or Bitten. They don't know what it's like to be hunted."

And now, finally, Henry looks over at me. It's actually quite startling how much Alivia looks like him. The same exact brow. The same lips. Jaw. The serious eyes.

If Alivia looks like him, I look like him.

"You have no idea how many of us are out there now, do you?" he says.

My stomach goes cold. It spreads like a wildfire, ripping through my veins, spreading clear to my fingertips and toes.

"What do you mean?" I ask in a breath.

Henry looks at me, and the longer he looks at me, the deeper I study him, I realize.

I've seen this man before.

Holy shit, I've seen him before. More than once.

My memory falls back, back to when I was maybe seven years old. I'd been riding my bike and, distracted by one of my neighborhood friends talking to me from across the street, I didn't see the rock in the middle of the road.

I hit it. I lost control of my bike, and a second later, I was skidding across the pavement. I'm sure the scream that came out of my lungs was impressive.

A man darted down the sidewalk. I didn't pay attention to where he had come from. But he was there, kneeling in the road beside me, pulling a handkerchief from his pocket and dabbing at my skinned knees and palms.

"There, there," he cooed to me, trying to calm my sobs. "It hurts now, but in a few minutes, you're going to forget all about it and you'll show off your battle wounds with pride."

I looked up at him, thinking it was a strange thing to say. But it still hurt and I kept crying.

"Let's get you home to your family, okay?" he said, offering a comforting smile.

I nodded. And I shouldn't have trusted a stranger so much, but I wasn't afraid of him for some reason. The man scooped me up into his arms, and I felt safe and I felt better. This stranger didn't have to ask where I lived as he carried me straight to my house and transferred me to my father's arms when he came to the door.

And then, my sophomore year of high school, something unexpected happened. Eli brought a friend with him to a family barbeque. He'd never done that before. But he said Henry was a friend from work, in town for a short visit.

He'd met my parents. He'd laughed with them. He'd joked lightly with Eshan. He'd talked to me about my school-work and what I wanted to be when I grew up.

I hadn't recognized him from so many years ago.

I didn't think it was important enough to store his name in my memory.

He'd been clean-shaven then. His hair had been so much shorter. He was kept and clean.

He looks so different now.

But I take in a sudden breath, realizing: this is my grand-father. And he'd checked in on me multiple times over my life, even if I had no idea who he was. But all along, I'd had family, and family friends making sure I was safe, and protected, and loved.

"You were there," I say, the words coming out breathy and quiet. I vaguely remember him saying something before, something important. But it feels kind of far away and distant right now. "As a kid. You...you were there. I remember you now."

There's a spark of a smile there now on his face. It doesn't fully form, but it tries to. "Alivia knew she could never, she would never risk exposing you to him." His eyes flick over to Cyrus for a moment. "But she loved you. She wanted to be sure you were safe and protected. That's why she sent Rath to watch over you. And I had to know, as well. I missed all of Alivia's life. And I hated that I couldn't be present in my granddaughter's life, either."

The Logan part of me wants to be snarky and bitter and

say that if he really wanted to, it wouldn't have been that hard to subtly make himself a part of my life, hiding who he was, just like Rath did.

But it's too late now. It doesn't really matter now.

I'm learning a lot about what kind of a man Henry Conrath really is.

"What did you mean?" I ask again, pushing aside nostalgia and memories. Henry said something really, really important. *You have no idea how many of us are out there now, do you?*

Henry blinks, looks out the window for a moment longer, and then turns away from it, going to the desk that sits against the far wall. There's a bag atop it. He unzips it and rummages around inside. "There are so many more vampires in the world than anyone would have guessed," he says. "A lot of them are coming out. Some are forced. There have been...displays, around the world. Proving to the world that we are real by making us go out into the sunlight and scream in agony. Or there have been fights, forced to the death, displaying their capabilities. There have been public feedings, and a whole lot of new Bitten created."

My breathing rips in my chest, a sharp, sudden thing.

No.

No.

The world is already turning into what we feared.

"There are already legions of people lining up to be turned by Born, chomping at the bit to become one of these new creatures the world knows exists now," Henry says as he continues rifling through his bag.

"But they've been outlawed," I say, and I know it sounds

stupid, but it still comes out. "Creating one is punishable by death, and has been for sixteen years now."

"None of the old laws matter anymore," Cyrus says. I look over at him, and he's staring at the wall, but I know he's not seeing the dirty and decaying surface. He's imagining this new world.

Humans are fascinated by things that are different. We stare in morbid curiosity. We gape. We study it. Sometimes we want to be it. We want to be different, even when we so badly want to fit in.

I can imagine the allure of being turned into a Bitten. Of having another vampire drain you of most of your blood. Of getting to the point where you're right on the verge of death. But the toxins released into your blood take hold instead. Your body changes. It doesn't die. It evolves.

Into something stronger. Something elusive. Something a little wild and dangerous.

And I can imagine the women that will flock to the Born men. The children they'll try to conceive. The methods and means that will instantly develop to make more Born.

The vampire population is going to explode over the next few years.

"It really is finished," I say quietly, looking up at Cyrus and Henry. "Everything, everything we ever knew is done. It's all going to change."

I don't know what Henry was looking for in that bag, but suddenly he closes it up again, coming away empty-handed. He turns, leaning against the desk and folds his arms over his chest. "The world is already a different place than it was yesterday. And it's going to change more and more, every day, from tomorrow, and the day after that, and the day after that."

I nod.

We always knew the ramifications of our exposure to the world would be desperate. But this...I couldn't have even imagined it. And I haven't even actually seen any of it yet.

The weight of this conversation is suffocating. It's filling the air with too much...just too much.

So I'm kind of grateful for the words that next come out of Cyrus' mouth, changing the subject.

"We need your help, Henry."

Kind of.

Henry's eyes flick from Cyrus' to mine. He's studying me, searching me over, like he can read signs of my demise off of my skin. And maybe he can. I am sweating. There were bags under my eyes this morning when I got ready to come here. Maybe he can hear my heart rate and know it's faster than usual for me.

"It has started happening, so soon after Resurrecting?" Henry asks in saddened doubt.

"Fifty-two days," I say. My words come out scratchy, because the burn in my throat feels so intense, even breathing feels painful.

Henry takes a step forward, and he keeps walking until he stops right in front of me, way in my personal space. He looks at me, nearly nose to nose. He looks at my skin, my eyes, my hair. I swear he's trying to study my DNA just by looking at the surface of me.

"I wonder why," he muses. By the way he says it, I know he isn't talking to me or Cyrus. He's thinking out loud.

"Your daughter said you have a cure." Cyrus' words come out slightly strained, and a little urgent. He's getting desperate, and I can feel time ticking down too, waiting for the bomb of my death to detonate.

Then how long would we have to wait before I am reborn once more? Where in the world will I wake up? How will the world look then?

Henry suddenly looks from me to Cyrus, even though we're still standing in such close proximity. He takes a step back, pacing to the other side of the room.

"You must be truly desperate to seek me out," Henry says. He stands in the shadows, and with the harsh light coming in through the window and the sunshades I have to wear because of it, it's difficult to see his eyes or read his expression. "Because I know that you know why I created it."

Beat. Beat.

The room is still for a moment, and suddenly, all these strings I hadn't thought about pull tight, connecting.

Henry was studying *Cyrus'* DNA. He was creating a cure for vampirism with it, specifically *Cyrus'* kind of vampirism.

Henry and Cyrus are enemies.

Henry created a cure he thinks will work on Cyrus.

If Cyrus is human, he could be killed.

He would die.

"Yes," Cyrus responds.

He stares at Henry. And I thought I knew the man I have loved for over two thousand years. I thought I knew his expression would be dark and penetrating.

But the look on Cyrus' face is open and desperate.

Cyrus can hold a grudge like no one else I know. But the past is gone for him right now. Whatever has happened between the two of them, Cyrus doesn't care anymore.

He just wants this cure.

He's different when the Queen is alive.

I'd been told this fact by hundreds of Court members and Royals over the hundreds of years. I know the darkness Cyrus is capable of. I've seen it. But I know I make him a different man.

"I will do whatever you want if you will only give it to Logan," Cyrus says. "She cannot die the death of a starving vampire if she is no longer a vampire. Maybe this..." he takes a step toward Henry, just one, and shakes his head. "Maybe this will finally break the curse, somehow."

Break it?

Break it?

What if?

What if it really works? What if I don't have to die in the burn and starvation anymore? What if this is finally, finally over?

But what happens when I'm human, when I live out a normal lifespan and die? Would I ever be reborn again? Would the cycle just start over? Or would that be it? Would it really be broken?

What if I die at the end of my human life, and Cyrus is left alone as an immortal? Alone. Forever?

"Do you think it would work?" I ask. I look at Henry hopefully. With a million questions. "Do you think there is any chance it would break the curse?"

I don't know what I want his answer to be. But there's

something in his eyes that tells me quite clearly that no, he doesn't think it will break the curse.

It will only put off this death.

"Have you ever tested this cure?" Cyrus asks, ignoring the fact that he didn't vocalize a response. "Are you sure it works?"

Henry doesn't look up at Cyrus, he looks back toward the window. "This strain? Only once."

"And did it work?" Cyrus asks, his tone getting a little more demanding.

"Yes," Henry responds, looking up at Cyrus. "It has been ten years since then, and he has resumed aging, just like he had never been a vampire."

"Who was it?" I ask, curious.

Henry's eyes are telling, yet reveal no secrets. He looks from Cyrus, to me, and then back to the window. "It doesn't matter. He was no one important to either of you. I simply did it for his family."

Yep, Henry is an annoyingly vague person. I think he likes being mysterious. But it's just obnoxious.

"If it works, what are we waiting for?" Cyrus says, stepping forward.

My grandfather looks over at me, and we study one another for a long moment.

My stomach is tied up in knots. My brain actually hurts. It's tired. Because it's running through a million scenarios, trying to figure out all the ends to this path.

And I just don't know.

Henry's eyes flick to mine. He pins me with those intense eyes. They're probing, like they can will the truth in me to the surface and read it from my skin. "What do you think of all this, Sevan?"

Sevan.

Logan.

I don't know who I am right now. Usually there are moments where I'm more one or the other.

But I think in this, I am the perfect blend of both.

I am...Segan. Lovan.

Cyrus eyes cut to mine, and I can feel his urgency. He doesn't understand why I am not answering right away. He sees no reason to hesitate.

But there are so many questions that I don't know the answers to.

"I want you to think about it," Henry says. He crosses the room, grabs his bag, and slings it over his shoulder. "The brain needs time to process information. You've been given a huge, life-altering choice. You need time to process it."

"What?" Cyrus demands with a growl as Henry walks toward the door. "You're not going anywhere."

Cyrus reaches out, grabbing Henry by the arm. But I reach out and touch his shoulder.

"Don't," I say quietly.

My husband looks back at me, and his eyes are brilliant red. I knew they would be.

But I also knew he would let Henry go.

"I will meet you back here tomorrow at noon," Henry says. Without waiting for another word from either of us, he cuts through the apartment and heads for the door. "Think about what you want for your future. What is best for this changing world."

We didn't follow him. So I only hear when he shuts the door, and his footsteps as he makes his way down those rickety stairs.

The silence between Cyrus and I is deafening. He takes three slow breaths through his nostrils, before slowly turning to fully face me.

"Why?" he demands. "Why did you do that? What if he leaves? What if he doesn't come back? What if he's changed his mind now? The man has a reputation for being unreliable and disappearing!"

My face is cold and numb as I look back at him. At the man I chose to be with. Over and over I have chosen to be with him.

If I don't take that cure, I *know* I'll come back. I'll be reborn again, and who knows, maybe this next time I'll get to live for a thousand years.

Cyrus is better when I'm with him.

He's going to need me.

What if this does break the curse? What if I *don't* come back?

"What about you?" I say quietly.

It's like he was a balloon and I just deflated him. His shoulders sag. The red in his eyes dies. His lips turn downward.

"What about you?" I repeat.

I see emotions well in his eyes and he looks away from me. He's wound tight. He doesn't know what to say. He doesn't know how to argue against that.

"Let's go back to our room and we can discuss this further," he says. His words are tight and clipped.

It's an aversion. It's a stall. Because he doesn't know what to say. I don't know what to think.

I don't protest. Silently, we leave the little apartment, we survive those stairs once more. We go back to our hotel room.

I didn't want to spend the rest of this day arguing with Cyrus. But in the end, that's exactly what we do.

He says he doesn't care what the outcome is, he'll take the risk. It's the way it should have been in the first place.

But what about him?

I can't leave him.

It breaks everything in me, but round and round and round we go with the same words and the same arguments.

Until finally, that night, we're both just emotionally drained and exhausted.

I lay down on my side of the bed and Cyrus on his. Our backs are turned to one another. We're out of words. We're just so damn tired.

So we don't say anything else.

CHAPTER 21

THE FLAMES AROUND ME ARE BURNING SO HOT. SO HOT THAT hot isn't even a word anymore. It isn't real. It could never fully capture what this burn is.

I burn and I crisp and I scream and cry.

With a gasp, I sit up in the bed, my hands going to my throat. My fingernails claw down my flesh, because it hurts, it hurts so bad and I need to make it calm down.

"Sevan," Cyrus says, and he's instantly at my side, his hands on my thighs.

I gasp. It's hard to breathe. Everything hurts. It burns. I suck in another deep breath, but it's so, so painful.

"Wait here," he says. I know there's panic in his eyes, but I can hardly focus on anything. I'm blinded by the burn. "I will be right back. I will make this better."

Then he's gone, and I'm alone with the burning in my throat.

I stagger to my feet and make it to the bathroom. I turn on

the water in the sink, desperate for anything to cool the fire in me. I put my mouth under the spout, guzzling water.

But it does nothing. If anything, it makes the burn worse.

With an angry hiss, I shut it off. Bracing my hands on the counter, I look up at myself in the mirror.

I shouldn't have done that.

I hardly recognize myself.

I wither when I'm in the final slope toward death. I literally shrivel. My skin all looks tighter on my bones. I look like I've lost twenty percent of my muscle mass.

And my eyes. They look sunken. There are dark circles around them. I look like I haven't slept in ten years.

I hadn't meant to fall asleep last night, but I did. After all the arguing with Cyrus, I was just exhausted.

Just one more evidence of what is happening to me. Being a vampire, I don't need that much sleep. I had slept so recently, too.

My nostrils flare as the burn in my throat intensifies. My eyes are bright red when I turn away from the mirror. I stalk toward the door, even though my knees wobble. I hardly have the strength as I walk across the room and reach for the doorknob.

I can't wait for Cyrus. I have to feed now.

But the door swings open just as I go to grab it. Cyrus steps inside with a terrified looking, wide-eyed man with a uniform on that says he works for this hotel.

My humanity is gone. I don't even care about what I'm going to do. I grab him the second Cyrus pushes him inside and I sink my fangs into his neck.

With a frantic moan, I grip him and walk us back into the

room. I hear Cyrus close the door, and he stands there watching me.

I pull and I pull. The man stands utterly still and silent, paralyzed by the toxins my fangs release into him. His blood is the best thing I've ever tasted. It's so sweet and so tangy.

But the burn. It says this is not enough. It's still too hot, still too wild.

"Another," I barely get the word out between pulls.

Cyrus knows exactly what I mean by that one word. He opens the door and leaves again.

I pull and pull again and again. I take his blood. It fills me up. There's the faint sensation of being full, but almost just as quickly, I feel my body burning through that blood. Like it evaporates inside of me. I use it up almost as quickly as I can consume it.

I pull, so greedy, but then there's nothing left. I suck out the very last drop.

With a frustrated grunt, I let his body fall to the floor. My human self is gone right now. I don't even acknowledge that I've killed a person. He might have had a family. He certainly had friends. He will be missed.

I ended a life.

But right now, I'm only impatient for Cyrus to return with another body for me to drain.

Exhausted from the effort of supporting the man as I drained him, I sink onto the bed. I lie on my side, closing my eyes.

Think of something else, I tell myself. Think of anything else.

Henry.

The burn.

The cure.

The burn.

Do I want to take it?

The burn.

Burn.

Burn.

I let out a frustrated and anxious sound, and two seconds later, Cyrus walks back in the door.

I instantly find my energy, but only enough to sit up. And my exhaustion must look evident, because Cyrus guides the woman to me. And I don't know what's wrong with her, but she doesn't even fight me as Cyrus sits her on the bed beside me, and I sink my fangs into her flesh.

It takes me longer this time to drain the body. My exhaustion is kicking in. Even sucking feels tiresome. So it takes me four minutes to drain this woman instead of the two it took to drain the man.

When I'm finished, I just let her body drop to the ground. I lick my lips.

The burn is better. It's just like glowing coals now, instead of a raging fire.

But already I can feel my body going through the mass amount of blood I just drank.

I'll be in pain again in just an hour or two.

Cyrus crosses the room again and kneels in front of me. He reaches up, caressing my cheek. "Better?"

I feel numb. Tired. But I force my eyes to find his face and focus on his eyes.

It was his eyes that I first fell in love with.

I nod.

He slides his hand around to the back of my neck and brings my forehead to his. "I'm so sorry," he breathes. There's so much pain and grief in his voice. I believe every syllable. "I'm so sorry that I did this to you, Sevan."

I reach up, lacing my fingers through his hair, but even that exhausts me.

I want to say that it is okay. That I forgive him. And I do. But I feel so awful right now. I feel so wrecked. I feel like death.

"Just hold me," I say. But speaking makes my throat hotter, makes it feel cracked and dry.

He nods. Carefully, he climbs around me. He tucks himself in behind me. I fold into him, and breathe a little sigh of relief. We fit perfectly against one another. Like he and I were molded to fit like this.

"Only two more hours," Cyrus says quietly.

My eyes find the clock. Only two more hours until Henry agreed to meet with us again.

A pit forms in my stomach. Because I have no idea what I'm going to do when we meet with him again.

THERE'S A STRANGE LOOK ON CYRUS' FACE AS WE MAKE OUR way back toward the apartment. I think that's hope in his eyes, but there's also fear, maybe. But those two emotions don't fully describe how he looks. I've never been good at reading people, so I can't tell exactly what it is he's feeling.

But I can't even focus on that right now. Not when the burn is back with so much force, it's all I can do to not grab every human who walks past me and drain every last drop of their blood.

I wouldn't have the strength. I can barely walk down the road. My knees shake. My hands tremble. There's sweat on my brow.

I could lie down right here in the street and take the world's longest nap.

We're two blocks away from the apartment when my knees give out.

A woman and her child who were walking by see how fast Cyrus moves as he catches me. They take a long look at the sunshades we wear. But Cyrus doesn't notice. He's whispering in my ear as he carries me toward the apartment. He's telling me he's going to make everything right. He's going to fix everything.

I like hearing his voice. I love hearing him speak.

But my head is pounding right now. Every sound he makes sends another wave of pain flashing through my brain.

I think of the death that is coming for me. It can't be far off. I think of how peaceful it is, once the dark takes over. I think of how quiet it is. It's comfortable, death.

I'm not begging for it yet. But it won't be long.

I hear the creaking of those stairs and we're rising. I worry about our combined weight being too much for them, but only in a very small corner of my brain.

The smell of abandoned space hits my nose and the world grows darker, to my every ounce of relief. Cyrus steps inside with me, and closes the door behind us.

"Everything will be okay," Cyrus coos into my ear again.

My grip on his shirt tightens, and I nod my head.

He can't make it better. This is death. This is the end. But I love him for saying it.

Even through my pain, I can hear someone back in that bedroom. Cyrus carries me and goes toward it.

Staring out that window once more, is Henry.

His hands are held behind his back. His shoulders are tense. He looks out over the water, staring out into the brilliant sunshine like it doesn't bother him at all.

Henry is a man of science, I remind myself. He's created a cure for the Bitten, a cure for any kind of vampirism. Who is to say he didn't find a way to fix his permanently dilated eyes so he can enjoy the sun again?

"The country of Moldova has become a mecca for vampires, overnight," Henry says. He doesn't turn away from the window. He keeps talking, almost as if he's thinking out loud. "Their government welcomed them with open arms and guaranteed they would be treated as with unique, high regard. And the state of Kansas is now crawling with thousands of vampires, all converging in the center of the States. The furthest point from any House, so they think they can get away with anything."

In my brain, I'm picturing a map, finding Kansas.

They fall under the jurisdiction of the House of Sidra, but they're nineteen hundred miles away from where it is physically located.

"The reports of the number of Bitten being created every day are astounding," Henry continues. "Thousands by the day."

My stomach feels sick. The Bitten are similar to the Born in that they drink blood. But they're not as strong as a Born.

213

They aren't as fast. They don't have the same kind of control over their thirst. And they continue to age. They grow old and die eventually.

But the worst part is the Debt. A newly created Bitten is compelled to obey its creator. They cannot say no. They would follow them to the ends of the earth. Kill anyone they were asked to. They would fight any war for their master.

It's the reason Cyrus outlawed their existence. They have no control. They can't help it.

Now there are thousands of them being created every day?

The human population could be hunted down and eradicated very quickly.

When Cyrus and I envisioned our exposure, we never pictured it going this way. We never thought of the mass numbers that would stoop to being Bitten in order to try and be like us.

I can't even imagine what the world is going to look like in a year. In five. In ten. I don't think it will even still exist in a hundred.

Moab and Lorenzo were successful. They brought us into the light. And they're erasing all the lines between Bitten, Born, and Royal.

We're all just predators now.

"I tried to stop it," Cyrus says, bringing me back into the present. He walks over to the bed against the wall and gently lays me down on it. "I did everything I could to ensure this would never happen."

Henry takes one breath, and turns partially back toward us. "That you did, Cyrus." His eyes are dark, and there are a million accusations in them. But also credit. "For all your faults, for all your bloody mistakes, you did try to keep the world safe from you."

My eyes slide back to my husband, and as if he can sense it, his meet mine. His lips are set in a firm line. His shoulders are tense.

I reach up, searching for his hand, and he gives it to me. His touch is gentle. Tender.

"I tried my best," he says. And I don't know if he's still talking to Henry, or admitting this to me. He falls to his knees, kneeling at the bed beside me. "I created something I could not control. In my thirst for knowledge, I cursed the world. I was selfish, in so many ways, for so many years. But I know now. All I ever wanted, all I ever needed, was right by my side."

He brings my hand to his lips and he gently presses them against the backs of my knuckles.

My heart flutters. He reaches into my soul, and for a minute, I swear he can just take me from this cursed, dying body and carry me forever. He can protect me. We can simply exist as one.

"This world is something different from the one I did not know I was creating," Cyrus continues to speak. He doesn't look away from me. I stare into those dark, dark green eyes. Green as the forest. Green as the deep parts of the ocean. "This is a new world. And I am so very, very old."

His words, they send a shock through my heart. Like it beats a little too big, suddenly. A little too hard.

A tiny shot of fear and adrenaline shoots through my blood at his words.

My eyes widen.

His do, too.

And I can feel it. It's a confirmation, that yes, this is what he's doing.

"I am done," he says only one second later. His head whips to the side, and he pins Henry with his gaze. Henry, who faces us, studying Cyrus with curious, surprised, doubtful eyes. "With all of it. With my quest for the incredible. With this species. With the crown. I'm done."

I...I...

I have no words. My heart thunders. I'm floating. I'm buried twenty feet under.

What he's saying...

Cyrus climbs to his feet, though he doesn't let go of my hand.

"You may say this cure will not do enough for Sevan," Cyrus says. "I don't know if you've even decided to help us. But I offer you a bargain."

"Cyrus," I say, but I don't know what else I have to say. I can only squeeze his hand, a question. *Are you sure?*

He squeezes back. *Yes.*

Henry doesn't move a muscle. He stands there with his hands folded in front of him, staring Cyrus down like he can read all of his truths from his soul.

"Give me the cure, Henry," Cyrus says. "I'm done with it all. Give me the cure. Save Logan. And we will walk away. From all of it. And you will never hear from me again."

I smell something in the air.

I feel it. It's cold. It's like death.

It's like life.

It's light and heavy.

It's the universe creeping in, coming to watch.

I feel it like it is a physical, real thing.

Cyrus stands a little straighter then, his eyes flicking around the room, and I know he can feel it, too.

Even Henry's eyes search the room.

There's nothing to be seen.

But we feel it.

"Give me the cure," Cyrus says. And this time, he's begging. His voice comes out desperate and quiet. "I'm done, Henry. Let me live out my life with my wife."

The room feels too quiet. Like every flow of air has stopped. Like the world stopped existing outside.

The entire world is holding its breath, listening to the words it has taken Cyrus two thousand years to find.

Henry takes three steps forward, and a fearful sweat breaks out on my upper lip. I don't know what he's going to do. I don't know what he's going to say.

He stops right in front of Cyrus, only two feet away.

"I can almost see you as a man right now, Cyrus," he says. "I can almost believe you are not only a heartless tyrant."

I feel desperate inside. I want to convince Henry that Cyrus is good. He is beautiful inside. He may be imperfect, but he is worthy of a second chance.

I take in a breath, but it's a mistake, because it only gives more oxygen to the fire inside of me. It sounds raspy. It sounds like death.

My husband squeezes my hand.

"Please," Cyrus says quietly, his voice filled with emotion.

And that word alone should be enough to convince Henry to do it. I have never heard Cyrus say that word to anyone but me.

"I just need one thing from you first," Henry says. His jaw is set hard, and he stares at Cyrus with such intensity, I'm surprised he is not a black melted pile of tar on the floor.

"Court had wanted to bring in a member of the Conrath family for centuries," Henry says. He does not look away from Cyrus, but somehow I feel his words are for me. "Not long before I moved to America, my wife conceived. She brought forth a son. We named him Nicklaus."

There is something familiar about this story in the back of my brain. Something back from my life as La'ei. But I can't remember anything other than the name.

"You took him," Henry says. "You tried to woo him with your castle and your willing human feeders, with the easy life."

I hear the pain in Henry's voice, and I know how this story ends, even if I was not around to witness it.

"And when he told you no, you killed him."

He's fractured. Broken. I hear it in Henry's voice. He broke a long time ago, and I don't think he ever put himself back together.

Alivia had a half brother she missed meeting by centuries.

I had an uncle.

"You killed my son." Henry's voice is little more than a whisper.

For the first time, Cyrus lets go of my hand. He shifts closer, nearly nose-to-nose with Henry Conrath. He takes both of the man's hands in his.

"I am sorry, Henry," he says. His voice is rough. As if it's been lashed with one hundred whips. "I am not a good man. I have been manipulative and selfish and a tyrant. I've taken what I wanted and used others to entertain myself. I am not a good man."

There are tears rolling down Cyrus' face. I have seldom seen this kind of emotion on my husband's face, and I've had two thousand years to study it.

"I lost my own son," he says. He's laying himself raw before Henry. Because Cyrus does not talk about our son. Ever. "I lost him even when he was a boy. Perhaps it was my utter failing as a father. So when I lost him, when I had to kill him, it ripped me to pieces. But I also felt relief."

It's a confession. A terrible truth.

But that's what it was.

A relief.

We were relieved when our son was dead.

"So I cannot feel your grief as I should have," Cyrus continues. "I took it too casually. But I have lost my wife, over and over. And with that pain, I apologize for taking your son from you. From the bottom of my heart. I am sorry, Henry."

Neither of us gets a chance to react.

With Cyrus' words, Henry raises his hand, and I don't even see the tip of the needle before he sinks it into the side of Cyrus' neck.

Cyrus gives a cry of pain as he sinks to his knees.

And there's this…blackness that rushes from Cyrus. It fills the room, swirling, circling. It rushes around us, searching for an escape. It seeps out the cracks around the windows. It rushes out the door. It sinks down through the floorboards.

I blink. I can still see everything. The floor, the walls, the bed. I can still see Henry and Cyrus. But there's this other… layer. That black. That dark.

As Cyrus screams, it pours out of him.

"Cyrus!" I cry, reaching a hand out toward him.

And where I was weak just moments ago, I feel strength rush back into me. I physically feel my muscle mass returning. The burn in my throat and my stomach are stifled.

I look at my hands, my arms, I feel my face, my eyes wide with wonder.

I feel it leaving me, too.

The dark. The blackness.

I can breathe.

I never knew there was a noose around my neck, slowly pulling tighter and tighter through every one of my lives. But it's gone now.

Vanished.

Cyrus suddenly collapses to the ground. With a scream, I'm instantly by his side.

"He only sleeps," Henry assures me.

And as I feel him, watch him, I do see his chest rising and falling.

I watch him, trying to reassure myself that he is, in fact, alive. He isn't dead.

I can't breathe. My organs freeze.

Because his smell changes. Just slightly. Just fractionally. But it changes.

It smells more human.

"Holy shit."

The words come out loud and harsh. They actually startle me and I snap my hand over my mouth, but with wide eyes, I look up to Henry.

"It's working," I breathe. "He's...Cyrus...he's turning human."

Henry meets my eyes and nods. "I developed it specifically for him. It will work. He'll wake in about thirty-six hours, and he will be human."

Human. *Human.*

Cyrus human.

Holy shit.

Holy *shit.*

Holy shit.

"I'm ready," I say, climbing to my feet. I step desperately toward Henry. "I want it too. Give it to me. This is our chance, Henry. To have the life we were supposed to have together. Give me the cure, Henry."

There are tears streaking down my face now. They're amazed and a little scared, and so incredibly happy.

Henry reaches into his pocket and produces a vial. It's filled with acid green liquid.

"Are you sure, Sevan?" he asks. "This. This is what you choose for yourself? For forever?"

Forever.

He says the word with absolute confidence. Like he knows.

And I know it, too.

Forever. This has to be my choice for forever.

Because Cyrus making that choice, saying all those words just a minute ago, he broke the curse.

His curse.

My curse.

If I take this cure, it's done.

I'll age. I'll turn into an old woman, and Cyrus will become and old man. And we will die eventually. And that will be it.

For forever.

"Yes," I say. And I smile when I do. I nod my head, and tears roll down my face. "Yes, Henry. This is what I want. More than anything."

I see my confidence reflected in Henry's eyes.

He gives me a nod.

He raises that vial with that green liquid.

And I give him one more nod.

And he plunges it into my chest, right into my heart.

A searing pain flashes through my entire body. Like all the heat of the entire sun was just shot into me. It's so big I can't comprehend even a tiny fraction of it.

So it only lasts a second or two before it consumes me, and I fall into the blinding white light and burn into nothingness.

CHAPTER 22

My body feels like it weighs six thousand pounds. My ears are mostly deaf now. My lungs quickly suck air in and out, desperate, craving it. When I roll over, every one of my muscles screams in pain.

I push my hair out of my face and blink my eyes open.

I'm blind now, too.

I kind of feel like I need glasses with a really strong prescription.

A dirty ceiling is above me. I feel a lumpy mattress beneath me. And as I roll, I feel a warm body beside me.

With everything I have, I roll toward it.

And there I find Cyrus.

His eyes are still closed, but his breathing suddenly picks up. His nostrils flare just a little bit.

I take in a deep breath.

Nothing. I smell nothing. I can't smell his blood. I can't tell if he's human or vampire. I can't smell anything.

Because I'm human again.

I'm freaking human.

"Cyrus," I say as a smile curls on my lips. I prop myself up on one elbow and reach for him with my other hand. I place it on his cheek, caressing his face. "Cyrus, wake up."

The breath comes harder from his lips, but his eyes don't open just yet. I pull myself up farther on the bed, and gently, I press my lips to his.

A kiss brought him back once before.

If we're going to step into this new life together, I want it to start with a kiss.

He lets out a breath, and I can't tell if it's filled with pain or desire—maybe both. But his hand comes to my hip, and I can tell it takes every ounce of strength he has to pull me toward him.

Cyrus kisses me, and even this feels different. This feels…real. This feels so grounded to the earth. This feels like the most natural thing ever. Like the entire universe formed so that just the two of us could have this kiss. Logan and Cyrus.

"Logan," he moans. And I can tell now, he's definitely in pain. He breaks the kiss, and his eyes squint in agony as his head falls back to the pillow. "Does your body feel like it's been buried six feet under an entire mountain for two thousand years, as well?"

I laugh. I'm not laughing at him, but I laugh.

"Cyrus," I say as emotions once more come to my eyes, and they don't even try to hold on. They slip down my face. "It worked. You're…we're human."

He groans, flopping onto his back, his face contorted with pain. "I forgot. This feels... I forgot what it felt like."

I roll over. I still hurt. But I feel myself adjusting. Slowly. It's remembering that this is normal. "It won't last," I say gently, brushing my knuckles against his cheek. "Does this feel better?" I lean down and press my lips to his cheek, kissing my way down his jaw. I find his neck.

"Almost," he says. Once more his hands wrap around me. They slip under my shirt, his skin touching my skin. "I think I'll be all better in an hour or so."

I smile wickedly. Even though I'm exhausted, even though I feel like I'm only moving at half speed, I climb onto my knees and carefully straddle his lap. I lean down, coming nearly nose-to-nose with Cyrus. My hair falls down around us, blocking out the light that doesn't bother my eyes one bit.

"Do you feel it?" I ask, my voice little more than a whisper.

He knows exactly what I'm talking about. I see it in his eyes. "I had forgotten the weight that settled into my chest the moment I took that cure for death," he says. "I had forgotten the tightness around my heart that has been there ever since I turned you against your will." He shakes his head. And we both take a deep breath at the same time. "It's gone."

I smile and nod. "You did it," I say softly. "You broke the curses."

The craving of human blood.

Him never being able to die.

Me having to die over and over.

It began with Cyrus' choices. They ended with Cyrus' choices.

"I promised you I would make it right," he says. He brings a hand up to my face, and softly, so soft and so soul-crushingly tender, he kisses me.

I love this kiss.

I love feeling tired.

I love feeling so utterly mortal.

I hear the footsteps only two seconds before they enter the room. The door pushes open just as I straighten up, but I don't have time to climb off of Cyrus.

Henry walks into the room. He looks moderately annoyed to find us in the position he does, but he ignores us. He carries two bags that look familiar.

They're the bags that Cyrus and I brought with all our things.

"The effects of the transformation will wear off in about twelve hours," he says. He sets the bag down on the desk. "You'll feel normal, if you even remember what that is, around then."

He's wearing all black. He almost looks...tactical. Like he's about to go out and do some serious spying or maybe some hunting.

"Henry, it worked," I say, in marvel, telling myself it's no longer my business what he's about to go out and do. A smile spreads on my face.

And a tiny one forms on his own. He gives just one nod, looking away briefly as I climb off of Cyrus. My poor husband pulls himself into a sitting position with a lot of pain.

Oh, it hurts to move. I pull myself to sit on the edge of the bed, facing Henry the same as Cyrus. It feels like I spent twenty-four hours at the gym doing the most intense workout imaginable, and now I'm paying for it with my life.

"Every day the world is growing more alien," Henry says. He once more goes to the window and looks out at the ocean. "There's now twenty-four hour news coverage of the war happening in Roter Himmel. No one seems to understand it really, none of the Royals have stepped forward to explain. But the world knows it's important. And they've confirmed one thing for us."

Henry looks back over his shoulder. "Lorenzo St. Claire is still alive."

My momentary happiness sinks in my stomach like a wet, cold stone.

Henry turns away from the window, blocking out most of the morning light. "I will hold you to your bargain, Cyrus," he says, staring at the man who is every bit still capable of being a King, but is no longer one of them. "You *will* walk away from the crown. But first you must return to Roter Himmel and ensure Lorenzo does not continue to take breath after everything he has done."

I hate all those words. Every one of them.

In my happy vision of the next few days, Cyrus and I would take some time to recover, and then we would disappear into the night. We'd go to Fiji. We'd take that trip we never got to take. We'd take off and live our happily ever after.

We'd get a damn honeymoon.

But the reality is that I knew it wouldn't be that easy.

I fought for that war in Roter Himmel. I can't just abandon it.

We have to see this through.

"Lorenzo will die," Cyrus says, nodding his head. With a lot of effort, he gets to his feet, and he meets Henry, eye to eye. "We will make sure he never takes another breath. And then you will never see or hear from me again. They will never find me, even if they look. I will keep my promise."

He extends a hand, and after a moment of consideration, Henry shakes it.

"Take a quick shower, get dressed," he says as he takes a step toward the door. "You two smell like you escaped death. I'm taking you to the airport. You're going back to Austria in one hour."

CHAPTER 23

THE WORLD AS WE KNEW IT REALLY IS FINISHED.

Security isn't just checking bags and walking through a screening booth anymore. They check eyes. They flash lights in them. Anyone wearing sunglasses is greeted by an entire security team.

We've only been on Lanzarote for three days, and even something as small as airport security has changed.

We land back in Austria and as we walk the short distance between the jet and the helicopter, the pilot gives us a narrowed look. I see his nostrils flare. He smells us. We smell human.

But he knows better than to ask. He doesn't say a word. He just bows to us, and welcomes us back home.

"I need an update on this war," Cyrus says. And that hasn't changed one bit. The confidence and command in his voice. He still sounds every bit the King he was.

"The numbers are dwindling, your majesty," the pilot

says as we rise through the air and take off over the mountains. "There's been a lot killed on both sides."

"Any estimates on the numbers left?" Cyrus asks.

The pilot shakes his head. "My numbers would only be estimates. It wouldn't help you any. I'm not down there in the action."

Cyrus nods, understanding. "Have there been any more Royals arrive to help?"

The pilot nods. "The House of Ellis and Zhang arrived day before yesterday."

Cyrus nods.

Twenty minutes later, the helicopter lands on the tower and we climb out. Hand in hand, we head into the castle.

I'm scared. I'm nervous. Once more my brain is going through a million what ifs. I'm trying to sort out the implications of everyone here figuring out we're human now.

Cyrus is in danger. I'm in danger.

And if we're killed here, trying to fight this battle, that's it. We're dead.

No happily ever after. No living out the rest of our lives.

"Cyrus," I say quietly as we make our way through the castle. "We have to keep our presence here as secret as possible. We're...we're targets now, really soft and fragile ones. We need to figure out a way to kill Lorenzo and get out of here."

Cyrus looks around, and his eyes widen, like he just realized what I said. It's been so long since he was mortal and fragile, he forgot that was normal.

He nods his head, and he changes course, immediately steering us toward our bedroom.

When we step inside, he goes straight for his bedside table and pulls out a cell phone. He dials a number and presses it to his ear.

Once upon two days ago, I would have been able to hear who was on the other line with Cyrus. But I can't anymore. My ears can only hear so much. And I can't tell who he's speaking to.

"I need you here," Cyrus says. "We're back at the castle. Come alone."

It was Mina he tells me when he hangs up. She was just headed back to the war when he called, she's turned back and will be here in two minutes.

Sure enough, 120 seconds later, there's a knock at the door.

Cyrus opens it, and pulls her inside.

She inhales a deep breath, taking in our smells.

"Impossible," she says, looking from Cyrus to me. Her eyes are dark, doubtful. Questioning.

"You have served me this long, Mina," Cyrus says, staring darkly at her, right back. He isn't intimidated. He isn't afraid. Even though she could kill him right now, and not even break a sweat doing it. "So, I am telling you, you do not ask any questions, because I will not provide any answers right now."

I see in her eyes that she doesn't like it. She wants answers. She wants to know why we smell utterly human after being gone a few days.

But she will obey her king.

She only bows her head a little in consent.

"We need updates," Cyrus moves on. "On everything.

Our numbers, Lorenzo's numbers, who has fallen. If there are any hits on Lorenzo's location."

Mina puts her hands on her hips. "We've lost at least half of the Court members," she begins with far worse news than I ever expected. "And probably half of the Royals who came, as well."

I swear, loudly, shaking my head and turning toward the window. It's shut. It's nearly evening, the shutters will automatically open when it's dark. So I turn back around, waiting for more bad news.

"Lorenzo has suffered just as many losses, probably more," she says. "They aren't skilled fighters, but they do have some training. We ambushed one of their cells this morning, which turned the tide in our favor."

"We will win the war?" Cyrus asks for assurance.

She nods. "I think so. We've pushed them back to an alcove with Maksim St. Claire's help, we've got them pushed back and cornered in an alcove in the mountains. I would say this will be finished by sunrise tomorrow."

That is good news. That is really, really good news.

Not that it matters. Really, we've already lost.

But at least we can punish those who have ruined our world.

At least we can stop them from enjoying their victory.

"What about Lorenzo?" I ask. I take a step forward, folding my arms over my chest.

She shakes her head. "He's hardly been seen since the stalemate. He'll slip in and out of battle, but never for more than a few minutes. He's still alive, somewhere."

He laid low for six hundred years, of course he'd be a slippery, sneaky little fox during the war.

Mina looks uncomfortable, and I can tell there is more news she doesn't want to share.

"What is it?" I ask. I'm suddenly nervous. I really don't want to hear what she has to say. But I have to.

"We've lost a lot of people," she says. She swallows. Her eyes drop for a moment to the floor, and I know whatever she has to say, it's going to be bad. I see it in her eyes when she meets mine again. "Dorian was killed this morning."

It knocks the breath out of me. I actually have to sit down on the bed.

Dorian.

My grandson.

The one who cared so much about family. Who had so many children. Who helped create the world we lived in. Who was so loyal and devoted. Dorian, who fought by our side in the original war. He stood with us and never wavered.

"Dorian is gone?" Cyrus whispers.

When you've been around someone for nearly your entire existence, when you've lived as family for nearly two thousand years, it's incomprehensible that that could ever change. It seems impossible that someone like him could ever waver.

Could ever die.

"He was fighting," she says. "Five of them took him down. He fought for our freedom and secrecy until the very end."

I can't believe it.

This is shock. I can hardly think. My human body can't process fast enough.

But it must.

We don't have much time.

"Mina," I say around the thickness in my throat. "We need your help. We're going to kill Lorenzo tonight."

THROUGH THE CRACK IN THE DOOR, I WATCH THE TWO OF them. Their words are muffled, I can barely catch any of them with my now human ears. Something about national recognition and working together on creating new laws that will affect the entire world.

I didn't expect it to be this easy. To set this trap.

It's a testament to Lorenzo's ego, and the desperation every government official must feel during this time.

You don't keep an entire town full of vampires secret for centuries without striking some deals.

Cyrus has had a longstanding relationship with the Presidents of Austria. He agreed to keep his people under control and quiet, and the government of Austria kept Roter Himmel off of maps, and no major flight paths dot our skies.

So Cyrus and I made a call. Within one hour, we had the President with us, and together, we came up with the plan.

He would meet with Lorenzo under the guise of forming a national alliance. He would play it up, the fact that the King and Queen had disappeared, seemingly abandoned this war. There was no one left to lead the vampires, except Lorenzo. They would strike an accord. Austria would grant him a free zone in Roter Himmel, if he would keep his people contained there and not interfere with the rest of the country.

It didn't really matter what the details were. It was all fake. It was merely a tool to draw Lorenzo out.

He came to the meeting place, a nondescript building in the next closest town. He brought guards with him, but Mina took care of them in a matter of seconds once Lorenzo was inside.

Now, I watch, waiting for Lorenzo to get comfortable enough for me to make my move.

Faintly, I hear footsteps, and turn to see Mina walking down the hall. There's blood splattered across her front, and she wears a satisfied smile.

She must be sure that the perimeter is really clear. There were apparently more than two guards keeping watch, but now there are none.

"We have operated in peace with Roter Himmel for a very, very long time," the President says. "Now everything is changed. How are you going to make things better than they once were?"

That's the cue. The both of us storm through the door. Mina is faster than I can see. One second she was at my side, the next she has Lorenzo in this head-arm lock with a stake pressed into his back.

"Thank you, President Steiner" I say as I walk into the room. I look over at the wide-eyed man. "You can go now. We'll take care of this."

The back end of this is so much more complicated than it looks. What it took to get him here. The snipers poised and ready. The bodyguards surrounding the place.

But on the surface, it works smooth as butter.

He nods. And he leaves without a word.

Lorenzo shouts obscenities at me, calls me every foul name in the book. But he can't break out of Mina's grasp. He can't move without driving that stake into his heart.

I take my phone out of my pocket. There's been a call going this entire time, the line connected with Cyrus. I put it on speakerphone and place it on the table between Lorenzo and me.

"Ego is so often the downfall of a thirsty leader," I say. I'm not speaking into the phone, even though I know Cyrus is listening. I address Lorenzo directly. "You might have taken the upper hand. You might have been successful if you weren't so eager to fall for our plan."

"But he came," Lorenzo seethes. "The actual president. There's a need for this." He nods his head, indicating the meeting he thought was real. "In every country. Thank you for the idea, Sevan."

I shake my head. "Maybe it could have been arranged that way," I say. I place my hands on the tabletop. "You could have brought our kind to light in a calm, controlled manner. You could have struck deals with leaders. You could have done this in a smooth and calculated way. But it's too late, now."

I shake my head and I swallow. "You've brought us into the world with fear and a million questions. The world is scared, and do you know how people react when they're afraid?"

Lorenzo's eyes narrow, his nostrils flaring. He's angry. He doesn't like what I'm saying.

And he's also just realized that I smell different.

I smell like dinner.

"I've been born into nine different families now, Lorenzo," I say. "I have loved so many people. So many family members. I have thousands and thousands of grandchildren. I know the value of family."

I take a step forward.

"I know that people make bad decisions," I say. "None of us are perfect. Greed is a common sin. But what you've done..." I shake my head.

"What I've done is beautiful," he says, fixing me with his glowing red eyes. "What I've done will change the lives of our kind. It has changed the world. And the world will forever remember the name Lorenzo St. Claire."

I shake my head. "None of the reports know your name," I say. And it's true. "Few of them even remember the name of Moab." I step around the table. I come face to face with him, still held immobile by Mina. "What they are all talking about are the incredible feats of King Cyrus. Of what he created. Of the secret he kept for over two thousand years. They are fascinated by his descendants and the classes of our kind and the war he fought long ago that made it that way."

It makes me sad. That every word I say is true.

I use them against Lorenzo. Because he's ruined everything, and he has to pay for it.

"No one will remember your name, Lorenzo," I say. "But the world will never forget the name King Cyrus."

Lorenzo snarls, bucking against Mina. He takes a gasping breath as the tip of the stake sinks into his skin. Much further and he'll be pierced in the heart.

"I don't want to do this," I say. I don't look away from

his wild eyes. "I believe people deserve second chances. But this. You don't get to live after you ruin the world."

On the cue, through the phone still sitting on the table, connecting us to Cyrus, we hear a horn blow. The horn signaling retreat. The horn only those from Court and the Royal line will know means to retreat back to the castle.

"No," Lorenzo says. His eyes grow wide. He's panicked. As a member of Court, he knows that sound. "What...what have you done?"

And as his answer, seven seconds later, there's the sound of a million shots being fired.

Ten miles or so from here, in the mountains where the battle was being fought, everyone at war was silently surrounded by the *actual* army of the Austrian government. They were armed with the most advanced technology.

We faked an invasion before. Matthias' army pretended to be from the Austrian government.

But this one is entirely real.

When Cyrus sounded the retreat, all Court members and all Royals left the battlefield, leaving only Lorenzo's children.

"That is the sound of the end of this war," I say. The sounds of gunfire stop, only to have a few more pop off here and there. "That is the sound of you not getting to see the world you wanted. That is the sound of your failure as the kind of leader our kind needed."

There's one last pop, and I can imagine the last of my half-siblings falling to the ground, dead.

There's a knot in my stomach. I hate that it has to come to this. But there's no other way.

"You failed, Lorenzo."

Mina shoves the stake forward, and Lorenzo's eyes grow wide as his heart is pierced. I see the panic in them, the horror, the regret that he wasn't smarter.

But then the light in them dies, and he's gone. His skin turns ashen gray even as Mina drops him to the ground.

Tears slip down my face. Because it might be over, but we didn't win. Everything is still ruined.

But this was the last war I will ever fight. This was my last problem to deal with as Queen.

This is the end of our era.

CHAPTER 24

THIS WE DID NOT PLAN OUT PARTICULARLY WELL. GETTING back together. What we were going to do once the war was finished, once Lorenzo was dead.

It's a testament to our long lives together that somehow, we both know to go back to the one place that is just us.

A tidal wave of relief washes over me when I pull our bedroom door open and find Cyrus inside.

He has a black bag in his hand and looks like I found him packing. But the moment he sees me, he freezes, his dark green eyes meeting my yellow-green ones.

"It's done," I say. And I say it just a little bit as a question.

"It's done," Cyrus says as a confirmation. He sets the bag down and crosses the space to me. I let him wrap his arms around me, pulling me into his chest. Emotion wells in my eyes as I press my face into the crook of his neck. I cling tight to him.

I was scared for his part of the plan. He would sound the horn of retreat. But he couldn't be seen. We couldn't risk the Court members and Royals seeing him, smelling how human he is.

Anything could have gone wrong.

But here he is.

I feel Cyrus. I feel his heart pounding against my chest. I feel the slight tremble in his hands. I hear his shaking breaths.

He feels it, so much more powerfully than I do. That this is the end. We lost. After two thousand years of keeping this secret, now it's ruined.

It isn't our secret anymore, I remind myself.

"Me and you," I say, feeling myself calm. "We're going to be okay."

He doesn't even hesitate. Cyrus nods his head. "I swear, I am going to give you such a beautiful life, Logan. We're going to be happy."

His words push peace through all of my veins, straight to my heart.

"Are you ready?" I ask.

He knows what I mean, and I'm a little disappointed when he backs away from me slightly to look into my eyes, and I see his answer is no.

"I have one last thing to take care of, *im yndmisht srtov*," he says. "I need half a day, and then we can leave this place forever."

I nod. Even though I don't like that idea. I want to go now. I'm ready to move on.

But I see in his eyes that whatever it is he has to do, he needs it.

"Gather our things," he says. He takes a step away from me and goes back to that black bag. "Anything you deem is important to keep. We will leave by tonight."

I nod. And he's in a hurry. Because he places a kiss on my forehead, and immediately slips out the door.

Pack our things, I think to myself as I turn to our bedroom. My eyes scan the room, thinking over what I value enough to take with us.

There's nothing. Nothing here holds any value to me. Not the safe full of expensive jewelry. Not the silk gowns. Not the expensive paintings that adorn the wall.

Except the one of Cyrus and I perhaps.

But I'll never forget those memories. They're all there, safe in my head, with the thousands of others.

The only thing I care about when we go out on the run is Cyrus.

As long as he and I are together, I don't worry about any other stuff.

But as I think about the unknown, when I think about being on the run a long, long time ago as Sevan, I go to our closet. I find two bags. I fill them with clothes. Practical, normal clothes that will be easy to blend in with. I grab toiletries.

I stash the bags next to our bedroom door and go down into the armory. I grab four stakes, two for each of us, and a gun for each of us.

The war may be over, but this new world feels far from safe.

I deposit the weapons in a bag as well and go for the door.

If we're going to disappear and start over, we're going to need some money.

The hidden treasury, that no one knows about besides Cyrus and I, is on the fourth floor.

I swing the bedroom door open and listen. I feel so damn deaf. Once upon a few days ago, I would have been able to hear nearly everything going on from this floor down to the third. But now I can't hear anything at all.

The castle is my home and has been for thousands of years. But for the first time, I feel scared in it.

For the first time, I'm in it as a human and I could easily be prey to the current occupants.

I slip down the hall. The first floor is the one place I have a little confidence, because no one occupies this floor except the two of us.

On the second floor, I slip down the hall of bedroom doors. I go straight for the one I know she once occupied. I don't even knock, I just open the door and slip inside.

"What-" Grace startles from the desk pushed up against a wall. She pushes her chair back away from the computer she was working on. But the moment her eyes land on me, they widen, and study me up and down.

"You can go home now, Grace," I say. And despite my fear, despite the tenseness in my chest, I feel myself smile. "Your services are no longer needed, and the future of this castle and everyone in it is now very uncertain."

Grace slowly stands up, never once looking away from me.

"How?" she asks, her voice quiet and rough. "Never..." she shakes her head. "Never has anyone gotten...better once I felt death coming for them. But you...you're free. The mark is gone."

It fully forms on my face now. I smile. I feel myself brighten. And I know I'll never see this woman again, and the world now knows much of what she knows, so it doesn't really matter what I say now.

"Cyrus always promised me he would fix it," I say. And I feel peaceful when I say the words. I say them as Sevan, but it's like she grows tired as she says the words. Like she's lying down for a thousand year nap. "He promised he would find a way to fix the curse. After all these years, it was his choice that set us free."

And with those words, I feel her. Like Sevan shut her eyes, and let her self go down. After all these years, she finally is free.

Grace has no idea what I'm really talking about. But still, she nods her head, like she grasps it, just a little.

"Go home to your life, Grace," I say, turning back toward the door. "Find someone to hold on to. Keep yourself safe in this new world."

"Will it ever be the same?" she asks.

I hate that desperation in her eyes when she looks at me. I hate that slightly accusatory look in it. But I deserve it. We—Cyrus and Sevan did do this.

"I'm afraid not," I answer her.

She doesn't respond. And I'm not very good at reading people so I don't know what she thinks of my answer. "The helicopter pilot will be on the roof waiting for you," I say, moving on.

And with one last look, I slip out the door, never to see Grace, the predictor of death, again.

My heart rate picks up as I creep back down the hall. At the top of the stairs, I wait, pausing and listening.

I don't hear anyone. If anyone were back at the castle, they'd be on the main floor.

So, with a daring breath of bravery, I dart down the stairs.

There is a back stairway, further in the castle. It's the one I should be using. But I'm curious. I want to know, even though I'm terrified.

So, I take the risk.

I hardly even look around when I get to the main floor. I immediately hook around to the next set of stairs, descending down to the fourth floor.

I didn't see anyone around. But I was also kind of too scared to look around. Fingers crossed, no one saw me.

Once I step down onto the floor of the fourth floor, I immediately head down the hall. I go past the kitchen, the meeting rooms. I set down another hall, and follow it for what feels like forever. Finally, I turn into a small room. It's only fifteen feet by fifteen feet or so. There isn't a single bit of furniture in it.

I go to the back of the room and press on one of the wooden floorboards. It pops up just slightly. I reach under it and find the latch. It releases, and a section of the floor lifts, revealing a door.

I check to be sure no one has followed me, and slip down into the small room beneath the floor.

It's maybe five feet tall. It spans the width of the room above it, and the walls are lined with shelves. There are stacks of money, in just about every currency in the world. There are also bars of gold, boxes full of silver coins. There's jewels, raw, uncut diamonds.

The castle has an official treasury, where we have a treasurer who takes care of the finances for the castle and sends out the checks monthly to all the Houses around the world.

But this stash has been personally built by Cyrus and Sevan. Saved specifically for an emergency occasion such as this.

I grab one of the bags on a shelf and begin stuffing it full of money. I grab different currencies. I fill the bag to the brim. And for good measure, because I have no idea what is to come, I grab a second bag and fill it completely full.

I really don't know how much wealth is in this room. But I'd guestimate I have around four million dollars between the two bags.

A million doesn't really take up all that much room. It's kind of surprising, really. I fit roughly two million dollars in each backpack.

Considering the poverty I've lived my life in since I graduated high school, it's ridiculous that I spend so much time considering if four million dollars is enough to get Cyrus and I by for the rest of our newly gained mortal lives.

In the end it comes down to the fact that I can't really carry any more than this. It'll have to do. So I zip the bags up, climb back up to the actual floor, lock the treasury back up, and sneak back out toward the hall.

Now I can hear voices coming from up above.

Some I recognize. Most I don't. But there are cries of pain. Cries of shock. Angry voices discuss the state of the world. Others talk gleefully about the eradication of Lorenzo's children.

I hear talk of them finding Lorenzo's body staked to a tree when they came home.

Mina has a touch of flair when she wants to.

But there are fearful talks about where Cyrus and I are.

They wonder about who blew the horn to retreat, thereby allowing the Austrian army to take out the children of Lorenzo.

Where is the King? Who else could have blown that horn?

Where is Sevan?

Everyone has a million questions. But I can't answer them. I can't let them see me.

Our time has passed.

I take the back stairs, the ones deep in the castle that are infrequently used. Silently, I slip past the main level and I slip into the shadows on the second.

I listen. Cyrus and I might be done with this world and the way it is. But I still care about these people. I still want to know.

They do a count. Where we were once just over four hundred members at Court, there are only 153 left. There had been approximately fifty-four Royals who came to Roter Himmel to fight in the war. Only twenty survived.

That is what chokes my throat.

There are 108 Royals around the world. Fifty-four

showed up to aide the crown. Exactly half. And exactly half ignored our call for help.

But it doesn't matter now.

I didn't think things could get worse.

But they do.

Those still alive line up the dead.

I watch as they carry his body through the doors. As they lay him down on the floor among the dead.

Malachi.

The last of our grandsons.

The last champion of the old world.

I cry alone in the dark. Tears slip down my face. They roll off my cheeks in heavy sheets.

My grandson. The man who was so focused and smart. The one who allied himself with world leaders and human Royalty. But he never let it go to his head. His ambitions were only for the safety of his kind.

Malachi was loyal to the end.

"I'm so sorry," I whisper.

No one in this castle can hear me. But I hope that Malachi can.

I can hardly breathe. I'm filled with so much sadness. I'm cracked with pain and fear. Everything is wrong. Everything has changed.

Through my grief though, there is a little voice that whispers: *I have a future.* It's totally different from what I imagined. But it is just my luck. It's not easy and pretty.

But I've still got Cyrus.

And across the world, I have a little brother that I promised I would return for when this war was over.

I think through, if there is anyone I should say goodbye to, here. But there isn't anyone, now that Dorian and Malachi are gone. They all might be family, but not in the same way.

I'm free.

Silently, I return to our bedroom. I lock the door behind me, and put the bags of money on the floor beside the others.

Exhausted, I lie on the bed, pulling my cell phone out. I text Eshan first.

War is over here. World has gone to shit, but we beat the bad guys. I'm coming back for you sometime in the next few days.

Next I text Elle. *I'll be back for my brother in the next few days. Thank you so much for taking care of him.*

It's the middle of the night in Boston. I don't expect a response right away.

So I lay my phone on the nightstand. I curl into a ball, pushing out every thought and fear for the future.

And I fall asleep.

CHAPTER 25

S OFT LIPS TRACE THEIR WAY FROM THE CORNER OF MY mouth, over my cheek, down to my jaw, and then to my neck.

I smile, but I don't open my eyes. I let my hands find his hair, twisting in its thick locks. I hold him close to me. His body shifts closer to mine and I hook one leg over him so he can't escape.

I feel him smile against my neck. But his body is relaxed. His breathing is even.

I let my eyes stay closed. I bury myself into his body and I lie there, feeling peaceful and protected.

"I love you, Logan," he says gently into my hair.

"I love you, Cyrus," I echo him.

The words are so simple. A man fell in love with a woman and a woman found a miracle that she fell in love with this man. They got married. They're going to live happily ever after.

"Did you get everything done that you needed?" I ask.

He nods. "It is all taken care of."

I sigh. It's done. We've done everything we can.

"I'm ready," I say, shifting and propping myself up on one elbow. I look down at my husband. "Let's leave. I want to get as far away from this place, this life as I can. I want to get away and just get on with us being us."

Cyrus caresses my face, and then raises his lips up to mine. "That's exactly what I want, my forever heart."

Together, we climb from the bed. We grab the last few things that weren't packed. We each grab a backpack and another bag filled with money to start our new life.

We both pause by the door though, not quite ready to leave. We both look around. At the massive bed where we've made love. At the window that looks out over the valley we called home. At the black crystal chandelier that hangs above us.

We made a lot of memories here.

We've loved here for a long time.

But I take Cyrus' hand in mine, and together, we walk out the door, and head for the stairs.

We're going to make memories somewhere else. We're going to love somewhere else.

Home was never the place.

It was always the person.

I can hear voices and chaos down below us.

But that's not our world anymore.

Those aren't our concerns anymore.

This isn't our reign any longer.

We walk up the stairs that lead up to the heli-pad. In the

dim evening light, we walk across the rooftop to the pilot who waits for us with the helicopter.

We load our bags.

We climb inside and strap in.

The wings of the chopper spin faster and faster. Just as we lift off of the ground, Cyrus reaches over and takes my hand.

We both watch as we lift off.

We're ready, we're excited for our future.

But we had a good life for so long here in Roter Himmel. We're both going to miss it.

So we watch it silently as we fly toward the mountains, and through the trees, our view of Roter Himmel disappears forever.

CHAPTER 26

"E<small>SHAN</small> P<small>IERCE</small>," <small>THE VOICE CALLS OVER THE SPEAKER</small> system.

I jump to my feet, clapping and screaming, and generally looking like a fool. But I really don't care. It's my brother I'm trying to embarrass, and I know I've succeeded when he gives me this little side look. But there's a little smile that curls on his face.

By my side, Cyrus stands, too, cupping his hands around his mouth and giving a holler.

As Eshan walks across the stage, takes his diploma, and shakes the principal's hand, his friends also give a whooping, hollering cheer.

It makes me happy that he has so many friends. That he hasn't let his tossed life get him down.

The kid is ridiculously adaptable.

I'm grinning ear-to-ear, so damn proud of that lanky kid and those gold cords around his neck.

I never thought I was ready to be the parent to my little brother, but it's been surprisingly satisfying.

He's a good kid.

Sure, he's snarky and sarcastic and he knows all of my buttons to push.

But he's brilliant. He's kind. He's exactly the kind of person this new world needs.

Eshan looks in our direction once more before he walks across the stage and goes back to his seat.

The room goes quiet when the next name is called. "Carl Rammet."

A kid with curly blond hair gets up and walks across the stage. No one shouts his name, no one cheers.

It breaks my heart. But I understand why the room is suddenly so quiet.

Carl is a Bitten. Him, and two other kids in the high school are. Everyone knows that they are. Everyone knows the choice that they made.

And everyone is terrified of those three kids. Even though they've kept their thirst under control. Even though they're leading seemingly normal lives.

How can you not constantly be afraid of someone you know could kill you if they go too long between feedings— and feedings mean drinking the blood of those just like you?

For another thirty minutes, we patiently wait for the commencement to end and then it's over. Just like that, the last three years of hard work and emotional distress over girl-friends and backstabbing friends is over.

We head outside, and out in the brilliant sun, we mingle with other families, human and Bitten alike.

No other Born are in this area, not that I'm aware of.

Eshan looks embarrassed as he walks across the lawn toward us. I can't help but grin ridiculously big. He just looks so grown up and accomplished in his graduation gown and cap.

"I'm so damn proud of you, E," I gloat as he walks to us and I wrap him up in a huge hug. "Honors, scholarships. Look at you being all big and important."

"Geeze, *mom*," he says dramatically. "Calm down a little."

It causes a little twinge of pain in my chest, him calling me mom. And I hate that they can't be here. I hate it even more that they aren't here because of me. Because of what I was.

Ethan and Gemma Pierce were cut out of this world way too early. This world needs good, decent people like them.

"Congratulations," Cyrus says, pulling his little brother-in-law in for a hug.

I love seeing the two of them together.

Maybe we messed something up along the way with our son—our son who turned so dark and so against us that we blotted out his name from our history, never to be spoken again. Maybe we are part of the reason why he turned out like he did.

But Cyrus is so good to Eshan. He understands him. He knows how to read him. He knows when to come down on him when necessary.

They really are like brothers, but also like father and son in the best way they can be.

"You ready?" I ask, checking the time on my watch. We really don't have much of it to waste.

"Just a second," Eshan says. "I just need to say goodbye."

I give him a nod, but tell him with my eyes to hurry up.

He darts off toward a group of friends. They laugh and hug and they're being so much more genuine right now than I've ever seen them. I guess that's what saying goodbye does to people.

As I watch them, Eshan with all those kids who have been in and out of our house for the past three years, I wrap my arm around Cyrus' waist and lean in on his shoulder.

"Thank you for everything you've done for him," I say. "He needed you. Just as much as he needed me. Maybe more."

Cyrus wraps his arm around me as well and rests his head on top of mine. "He's family," he says. "He's…"

He doesn't finish his sentence. And I can almost imagine the words going through his head.

He's the son I wished we had.

A minute later, Eshan darts back over and says he's ready to go. So together, as a family of three, we head for the car in the parking lot.

It's a nice car, but nothing too flashy. Nothing to draw too much attention. We climb inside, and Cyrus points us back toward home.

I watch the landscape as we make the ten-minute drive. There's huge live oak trees and Spanish moss hanging from them. There are beautiful flowers here and there. The houses are old and beautiful.

I hate the humidity. I can't always understand the accents.

But I have loved our time here in Foley, Alabama.

It's safe here. It's quiet. There aren't problems like they're having in the big cities with the Born and the Bitten. We're as protected as we can be here. We're only a few hours away from the House of Conrath if needed, but far enough away we're out of the business of vampires, away from the possibility of being found and discovered by individuals who would recognize the two of us. Those who are looking for and hunting for Cyrus.

We pull up to our house, a beautifully restored home that was originally built in 1801. It's old. Kind of like us.

The minute we walk into the house, Eshan darts up the stairs, stripping off his graduation gown. I hear him upstairs rifling through his things, checking last minute for anything he's going to need.

"Are you sure you can handle this?" Cyrus asks, lingering in the foyer with me. "After three years, you're ready to just let him take off on his own?"

I smile as I step forward, wrapping my arms around his waist. A wicked smile grows on his lips as he looks down at me.

"Are you kidding?" I say, teasing him with my eyes. "I'm ready to finally have that honeymoon. Eshan's a big boy. I'll only worry about him once every five minutes now, instead of every two."

Cyrus shakes his head at me, but tilts his head down and presses a kiss to my lips.

Footsteps thunder on the stairs and Eshan rounds into the foyer just as I open my mouth to let Cyrus' tongue inside.

"That, I will never miss," he says in disgust. He hardly

even looks at me as he walks right past us and into the kitchen. I hear him dig through the pantry, and I'm pretty sure I hear him dump half of it into his already stuffed backpack.

We talk, reminiscing on the past three years as we drive to the airport. On his soccer games. On the school dances he was too chicken to go to his junior year, and finally got the nerve to go to his senior.

We've had a good life here in Alabama.

We've managed to lay low. To stay away from the insanity of the world.

But now Eshan's going to join it. He's jumping right into the middle of it.

We arrive at the Pensacola airport fifty minutes later. And it finally hits me. Emotions tug at my eyes, pull at my heart-strings as we walk him to the security gate.

"You sure you got enough underwear, or whatever?" I ask, trying to think what mom would have said in this situation.

"Are you serious?" he asks, laughing, adjusting the strap of his backpack.

I laugh and shake my head. "If you have clean underwear is no longer my concern," I say, stepping forward and pulling him into a hug.

"All you need is seven pair," Cyrus says. "One for each day of the week, right?"

Eshan laughs, letting go of me and hugging my husband. "Exactly. And then you can just turn them inside out and you're good to avoid laundry for another week."

"That is disgusting," I say with a gag.

It's a good laugh. But really, we're all having a hard time with this goodbye.

"Well," Eshan says, adjusting that strap again. "I only got twenty minutes."

I nod, ignoring the emotions that well in my eyes. "Okay," I say. "We'll call you in a week and let you know where we are."

Eshan nods.

"I'm proud of you, Eshan," Cyrus says. And no one could doubt his sincerity if they looked in his eyes. "You're doing an incredible thing. I don't think there's anyone more quali-fied. You're the kind of leader we need in this new world."

A scuffle to our left draws everyone's eyes. Five police officers tackle a man whose eyes are suddenly glowing red. They break out their stunners, designed specifically to take down vampires.

They aren't prohibited from traveling on airplanes, but one wrong look and they're taken into custody of the VBI— the Vampire Bureau of Investigation.

It's a common sight, one I fear will lead to intervention from the Crimson State, formerly known as the state of Kansas, where fifty percent of the United States vampire population has moved to and declared their own territory, with their own rules and government.

"Do good things, E," I say, hugging him one last time.

"Promise," he says.

And then I let him go. He gives me one last smile, and then heads to security.

I watch him until he's gone, holding hands with Cyrus.

After doing amazing in school, considering all the adjustments he had to make, Eshan got a revered apprenticeship with the International Vampire Peace Alliance. They're an independent agency that formed a year after the exposure. They aren't tied to any government agencies, because those proved to be a chaotic nightmare within six months. They're a group of leaders and citizens who work with prominent vampire leaders, some Royals and House leaders, some who have big family ties, or are simply individuals that others flock to.

He'll spend the summer there helping make the world a better place. And then in the fall, he's going to the new Integration University in Chicago.

My brother is going to help make the world a better place.

I watch as he disappears through security. He gives one last wave, and then he disappears toward his gate.

"You ready?" Cyrus asks.

I nod.

We return to the car, but only to grab our own bags hidden in the trunk.

Eshan knew that we were going to be leaving Alabama soon after he left, but he didn't realize that we were taking a flight only an hour after his own.

We've been based in Alabama for nearly three years now. But much of the world recognizes our faces from those news reports Moab did, exposing us and our kind to the world. To stay safe, to stay hidden, we have to move. We have to go underground again.

It's time for a freaking honeymoon.

I'm so ready for Fiji.

We make it through security without issue, and we head to our gate.

I look around at all the couples as we wait to board. We're obviously not the only honeymooners.

But that doesn't deter Cyrus from taking my hand and pressing his lips to the back of it. I look over at him and meet his smoldering, dark green eyes.

It was his eyes that I first fell in love with. All this time later, I still fall in love with them, every day.

"I'm going to give you the life I promised you," Cyrus says, his lips brushing against my skin, sending flashes of heat through my core. "We're going to be happy, Logan."

I smile, leaning forward. I touch my lips to his. "I am happy," I say quietly. "I love the life we have had."

He reaches a hand up, brushing his fingers along my jaw as he kisses me, deeper. Longer.

After all this time, it's finally our time. Time for us.

No more fighting. No more leading. No more making rules and laws. No more balls and politics and walking on eggshells.

It's just now.

It's our time.

Logan and Cyrus. Until the end.

CHAPTER 27

EVEN ALL THE WAY OUT HERE, IN THIS REMOTE CORNER OF the world, two miles off shore of the main island, we manage to pull together a birthday party.

There aren't a lot of us here. It's me and Cyrus. It's Eshan. It's Elle, and her very surprisingly human husband Lexington, and their three kids. It's Amelia and Trevor and their two kids. It's Alivia, but she's only here because of me. It's not Ian Ward.

We sing the classic rendition of Happy Birthday, and Cyrus sits at the head of the table with the German Chocolate cake in front of him, the candles dancing on top of it.

I smile at him as we sing, and my heart flutters.

There are crow's feet developing around his eyes. Little flecks of salt and pepper are showing along his temples.

He's just growing hotter with every passing year.

He might be thousands of years old, but physically, he's thirty-seven today.

His actual birthday got lost a long, long time ago, and time wasn't measured in the same way back then. So he picked one. The day that the war ended in Roter Himmel and we started our new life.

September nineteenth.

Cyrus is thirty-seven. He spent over two thousand years stuck at twenty-seven.

I cut the cake and everyone is happy and relaxed and together in the most beautiful way as we eat the cake and ice cream.

I watch them, marveling at the normalcy we've maintained when the world has turned into such a dark and chaotic place.

But I don't want to think about that now.

I want to think about Elle and Lexington, my aunt and, I guess, uncle. I want to watch their bickering and teasing kids who are turning into adults—Aster, George, and Penny. I'd rather laugh about Cyrus teasing Alivia, and her getting all flustered about it.

But the TV is on in the background, and the satellite channel changes to the news.

I sit on the hearth of the fireplace, and when the next news story pulls up, my eyes lock on it.

It's quiet, not very loud, and no one else is here in the living room, so I'm the only one that hears it.

"Today marks the ten year anniversary since the commencement of the battle at Roter Himmel." The woman with black hair and dark eyes gives the report like she's talking about something normal, and not something that changed the entire world. "It also marks the day that the world's largest game began."

A picture fills the screen.

It's of a piece of paper staked to the front doors of the castle with a knife. On it is elegant and careful handwriting.

"On this day, ten years ago, the hunt for the Crown of King Cyrus began, marking the disappearance of the man who created the vampire race, and his wife, known as Queen Sevan."

The picture zooms in, and the words become clearer.

"The hunt has taken Born, Bitten, even human alike on what seems to be a wild goose chase from one end of the earth to another. So far, any attempts to find the Crown of King Cyrus have been unsuccessful."

Now the words are easy to read.

They're there, clear as day, written in Cyrus' hand.

A MAN WHO VENTURES INTO IMMORTALITY FOR HIS OWN GAIN AND GRANDURE WILL FIND HIMSELF ALONE, OVER AND OVER AGAIN. A MAN WHO USES IT TO BETTER HIMSELF AND THE WORLD AROUND HIM IS A MAN WHO WILL FIND HIS LIFE IN HIS IMMORTALITY.

AS THE END OF MY WORLD ARRIVES, AND WE FIND OURSELVES AT THE START OF A NEW ONE, I REMOVE MY CROWN. MY ERA HAS CONCLUDED.

THIS IS MY FINAL GAME.

THE FINAL GAME OF KING CYRUS.

THE WORLD LOOKS TO A LEADER WHO WEARS A CROWN.

BUT FIRST IT MUST BE FOUND. ONLY THEN WILL MY CREATIONS HAVE A TRUE KING OR QUEEN.

A LEADER MUST BE KIND. A LEADER MUST BE WISE. A LEADER MUST BE EVENHANDED.

THE WORLD IS LARGE, THE WORLD IS COLD. AND IN THE HEART OF DARKNESS, IN THE HEART OF HELL, THAT LEADER SHALL BE CROWNED.

At the bottom of the letter, there is a picture of Cyrus' crown drawn.

I never knew what Cyrus had to take care of, our last day in the castle. I hadn't guessed what he'd had in that bag before he disappeared.

Even I have no idea where the crown is hidden. I don't care to ask.

Cyrus has always loved games. He has always loved to watch people scramble to figure out his puzzles.

Of course he had walked out of that world with the biggest one yet. The one that would set the entire world into a frenzy.

The hunt for the crown of King Cyrus.

I smile as I walk back into the kitchen, and set my plate on the kitchen island.

Ignoring the guests that are enjoying their cake at the table, Cyrus joins me, sliding a hand into my back pocket before leaning down and kissing my lips.

"Thank you for the lovely birthday surprise," he says.

I turn, wrapping my arms behind his neck. He tips down, pressing his lips to mine.

I forget that we're surrounded by friends and family. My

fingers lace into his hair and his grip on my back and waist tightens, claiming me as his forever.

Against his lips, I smile. "Anything, *im yndmisht srtov*."

THE END

ACKNOWLEDGMENTS

I really can't quite believe that I've been in this world for this long, and I also can't quite believe that this is the end. I have loved being in this Universe, as evident by the fact that I couldn't leave it for such a long time.

I need to thank three people in particular who got me through to the end: Sarah, JanaLee, and Lauren. You have each helped me through all of these books and you've been so willing and happy to do it. I can hardly express how much I appreciate all of you!

Thank you to my Street Team who have done so much work in helping spread the word about these books. You are all my friends and I love you for everything you do!

Thank you to you as the reader. If you're reading these

words, you are the reason why I can keep writing. Thank you for believing in me and for trusting me with your time. I hope I can create more worlds that you will love as much as this one.

ABOUT THE AUTHOR

Keary Taylor is the USA TODAY bestselling author of over twenty novels. She grew up along the foothills of the Rocky Mountains where she started creating imaginary worlds and daring characters who always fell in love. She now splits her time between a tiny island in the Pacific Northwest and Utah, dragging along her husband and their two children. She continues to have an overactive imagination that frequently keeps her up at night.

Made in United States
Orlando, FL
16 December 2022

26801595R00168